WITCH SWITCH

Lucky 13

Be Careful What You Wish For

Gone with the Witch

Witch Switch

TEEN Witch

#4

WITCH SWITCH

MEGAN BARNES

SCHOLASTIC INC.
New York Toronto London Auckland Sydney

ISBN 0-590-41299-X

12 11 10 9 8 7 6 5 4 3 2 1   9/8 0 1 2 3 4/9

Printed in the U.S.A.   01

First Scholastic printing, April 1989

Chapter 1

Sarah Connell watched her sister, Nicole, standing at the end of the high diving board, staring down into the rippling blue-green depths of the Waterville High swimming pool. The Waterville girls' team was far ahead of its nearest rival, Grantley High, and Nicole's own individual scores were the highest of the day.

Sarah knew that Nicole was so far ahead, that no one could possibly overtake her. All she had to do was get into the water any old way at all. She could jump off the board and still win.

But it wasn't like Nicole to take things easy. She was a perfectionist and always wanted to do her very best.

From her seat in the poolside bleachers, Sarah was studying her older sister intently, her mind reeling with a confusing mixture of emotions. She felt nervous on Nicole's behalf and proud of her, too. But she also felt a little tug of envy.

Sometimes it seemed to Sarah that she spent a good part of her life sitting on the sidelines, watching Nicole perform. Nicole wasn't just the star of the girls' diving team. She played tennis, too. And she was a member of the Waterville High cheerleading squad. What's more, she was pretty, popular, and a good student.

Not that Sarah was ugly. She had warm brown eyes flecked with gold, and long, naturally wavy chestnut brown hair. Most of the time she was satisfied with her looks. But Nicole was blonde with china blue eyes and a naturally slender, long-legged figure. That was a combination that was guaranteed to get attention, especially from guys. Probably, every girl has secretly wanted to be a blue-eyed blonde at one time or another, Sarah thought, if only just to know what it feels like. Maybe blondes really do have more fun. Sarah sighed and shook her head, trying to drive her envious feelings away.

Her best friend, Micki Davis, who was sitting next to her in the bleachers, smiled and patted her arm encouragingly. "Don't worry," she said, "Nicole will be okay. I'd take a long time, too, if I were up on the high diving board."

"I know she'll do it," Sarah told Micki. "It isn't that. It's just that sometimes I wish Nicole weren't quite so perfect."

At that instant, Nicole made her move. She got a good spring and launched herself high into the air. Then she went into her tuck easily and began turning. One half revolution. Another half. Then a third.

But when the time came to straighten herself out, Nicole's timing was off. For once, she didn't look like a graceful swan. She looked more like a ridiculous little frog, her legs wide apart, her feet splayed out at an odd angle as she struggled to regain her equilibrium.

Nicole entered the water safely, but just awkwardly enough to cause a huge splash.

"Thar she blows!" some joker in the stands called out.

There were a few scattered giggles from the spectators, mixed with gasps at the unexpected sight of Nicole Connell looking silly.

Micki shot Sarah a suspicious glance. "You did that!" she said accusingly.

"I did not!"

But Sarah couldn't quite work up a genuine look of indignation. "If I did, I didn't mean to. Honest. It was an accident."

A couple of guys sitting in the row in front of them turned around and stared at Sarah, obviously puzzled by their conversation.

Sarah nudged Micki and motioned for her to be quiet. "Not here," she whispered. "We'll talk about it later."

The last thing she needed was for Micki to blurt out her secret in front of complete strangers! Still, Sarah couldn't help wondering what those guys would say if only they knew that she, Sarah Connell, was a witch!

Sarah hadn't known herself that she was a witch until a while before, on her thirteenth birthday. And even now, there were still times when she found the idea hard to get used to. Having supernatural powers could be lots of fun. Sometimes she knew what people were thinking. She could travel backward in time and make wishes come true. She knew she shouldn't do anything bad, like changing the school principal into a warthog or cheating on a test. But being able to make objects move just by thinking about it certainly came in handy when it was time to clean her room!

Luckily her aunt Pamela, who was a grown-up, senior witch, was around to give her advice. But Aunt Pam couldn't be at her side all the time and, so far, Sarah had made a few embarrassing mistakes. There was the awful mix-up when she had made Cody Rice fall in love with her, for example. Her love potion had worked too well, and Cody had turned into a moony, lovesick bore. Then there was the time she had accidentally made Waterview High disappear. What a mess *that* had been!

Ruining Nicole's dive was another miscalculation. I've got to remember to be careful what I wish for, Sarah reminded herself mournfully.

Nicole's score for her last dive was really low, and Sarah waited anxiously for the judges to tally up the final standings. After what seemed an eternity, the voice of the head judge came over the loudspeaker:

"The runner-up for the individual trophy is Tracy Easton of Grantley. And the winner is Waterview's Nicole Connell."

"Way to go, Nicole!" Micki shouted.

Sarah felt a flood of relief washing over her. "Let's get out of here," she whispered, "before I cause any more problems."

On the way out of the gym, Sarah and Micki ran into Tina Jordan.

"You're just who I was looking for," Tina told them. "My mom has to take Tank out to the mall to get some school clothes, and I thought maybe we could hang out there for a few minutes while they're shopping. She'll give you two a ride home if you want to come along."

"Sounds good to me," Micki said.

Sarah nodded. Tank was Tina's brother, and even though he was only ten years old, he was as stocky as Tina was slender, and almost as tall. Sometimes Sarah wondered how it would feel to have such an unflattering nickname.

Tank didn't seem to mind, but he wasn't too happy about Tina and her friends coming along to the mall. "I don't want a bunch of girls watching me shop," he protested as they piled into the backseat of the Jordan station wagon.

Mrs. Jordan looked cool and unruffled. Like Tina, she had a flawless, chocolate-toned complexion and striking, wide-set brown eyes. "They're not coming into the store with us," she assured her son.

"We wouldn't want to," Tina put in. "We've got better things to do than stand around watching you try to find a pair of jeans that fit you."

"Tina, don't talk to your brother like that," Mrs. Jordan warned.

But Tank was capable of defending himself. "That's fine with me," he shot back. "I wouldn't want the clerk to see what an ugly sister I've got."

Mrs. Jordan ignored this crack, and Tina

looked at the other girls and made a face. "Do either of you have any plans for this weekend?" Tina asked, changing the subject.

"Not me," Micki said.

They both looked at Sarah.

"Huh?" Sarah hadn't heard a word of the conversation.

Tina giggled. "Earth calling Sarah. Come in, wherever you are."

That wasn't so funny at the moment. Sarah's mind really had been a million miles away. Or rather, floating back in time, trying to figure out if what had happened to Nicole really had been an accident. Maybe she *had* wanted to sabotage Nicole's dive, and was just feeling too guilty now to admit it.

"Tina wanted to know if you're doing anything this weekend," Micki reminded her.

"Oh." Sarah shook her head. "Mom and Dad are going to visit my uncle Paul and aunt Sylvia. But us kids can't go because they're leaving tomorrow morning. And naturally Dad won't let us skip a school day."

Tina let out a low whistle. "Does that mean that you and Nicole and Simon will be all alone in the house? Your folks are awfully trusting."

"That's because they know Simon," Sarah explained. "He may be only seventeen, but he's stricter than they are. I think he's some kind of authority freak. He loves giving orders to Nicole and me."

When they got to the mall, Tina practically dragged Sarah and Micki in the direction of Carrie's Casuals, her favorite store. Carrie's always had the most outrageous window displays at the mall, and today was no exception. The store's main window featured a Yamaha cycle that had been completely disassembled. Standing amid the clutter of chrome handlebars, tires, and miscellaneous sections of engine was a cool-looking mannequin wearing a mini-length lavender sundress with a gold-toned belt draped low over one hip.

"That dress would be perfect with my new sandals," Tina said dreamily. "But I look awful in pastels. I wish they had that style in some color that was really hot. You know, like shocking pink."

"They will," Sarah said a bit too quickly.

"I don't think so," Tina told her. "I already checked the last time I was here."

Sarah visualized the pastel sundresses hanging on the rack inside the store. Then she blinked hard and visualized the same rack again, this time with a hot pink dress in Tina's size mixed in among the baby blue and lavender ones.

"Why don't you check again?" she urged.

Tina shrugged. "Okay. What've I got to lose?"

When she had disappeared inside, Micki turned to Sarah. "Are you sure this is a good idea?"

Sarah smiled. "What harm can it do?" She was starting to feel good about her special powers again.

Seconds later, Tina came out of the store, clutching a plastic shopping bag. "I'm glad you made me check," she told Sarah. "I found just the color I wanted. And the salesgirl didn't even know she had it. You must be psychic or something."

Sarah smiled knowingly, and the gold highlights in her brown eyes seemed to stand out just a little more than usual.

They checked out the windows of the other shops on that level and then stopped for cherry Cokes at Burger Benny's, where Nicole worked part-time on weekends. Nicole's boyfriend, Derek, and a couple of his friends were just on their way out. As he passed Sarah, Derek nodded in her direction and grunted a greeting. "Huyay," he said. Or at least that was how it came out.

Micki waited until he was safely out of sight then pretended to swoon. "What a hunk!"

"He's nothing special," Sarah said.

"Girl, you must be blind," Tina said. "That cleft chin of his is really sexy. Besides, he has a great body. He must work out a lot."

"I guess so," Sarah conceded. "But sometimes I think he's trying too hard to imitate Sylvester Stallone. Did you hear how he talks? Besides, he treats me like I'm about five years old."

"Why," Micki asked. "What does he do?"

"It isn't so much anything he *does*," Sarah said. "I just get the impression that he thinks of me as a baby."

"I think you're imagining things," Tina put in.

"That's easy for you to say. You don't know what it's like to be the youngest in the family. Simon thinks he can order me around. And sometimes Nicole is even worse. No matter what I do, Nicole has already done it first and better. It isn't easy to follow her act."

"Maybe," said Tina, "but being an older sister isn't easy. Mom lets Tank get away with all kinds of stuff. I'm always supposed to set an example."

"It isn't that way at our house," Sarah insisted. "Nicole isn't under any pressure. No one *forces* her to wear plaid skirts and cardigans. No one *told* her she has to be little miss perfect."

"Okay, have it your way," Tina said. "But there's this saying my Mom always quotes: 'You don't really know a person until you've walked a mile in her shoes.' "

Micki laughed. "That could be awfully uncomfortable. I mean, what if your feet are size eight and the other person's shoes are six-and-a-halfs?"

"You're not supposed to take it *literally*," Tina said, exasperated.

Sarah didn't say a word. But Tina had certainly given her something to think about.

Chapter 2

On the way home from the mall, Sarah made up her mind to be extra nice to Nicole that evening. She was feeling guilty about what had happened at the diving meet and for criticizing her sister in front of Tina.

But being nice to Nicole wasn't going to be easy. Her sister was in a rotten mood.

Before Sarah had even put down her books, Nicole charged into the living room and started waving an empty plastic bottle under her nose. "You used the last of my shampoo again," she said accusingly. "How could you do that when you know this is the only stuff that gets the chlorine out of my hair?"

"I didn't use it," Sarah retorted. "Anyway, there's a spare bottle in the storage compartment under the sink." Her knowing that had nothing to do with magic. She had just happened to notice the shampoo that morning.

Dr. Connell's frowning face peered out from behind his newspaper. "I had double office hours today to clear my schedule for the weekend," he announced. "Plus Jimmy Regan tried to set fire to my waiting room again. But I expect my patients to cry and cause trouble sometimes. Any pediatrician expects that. They're only kids. You girls are old enough to know better."

"I'm sorry, Dad." Nicole's voice turned to sugar. She went over to their father and gave him a hug. "We didn't mean to bother you."

Her father returned the hug. "That's okay, Princess."

Sarah could hardly believe it. Nicole was the one who had started the argument, and now she was getting all the attention. It just wasn't fair! Disgusted, Sarah went out to the kitchen and worked off her anger helping her mother set the table.

Dinner that night was steak and mashed potatoes with gravy, an unusual menu because Dr. Connell was always trying to figure out ways to get his family to eat tofu, bran, and other strange foods that he thought were good for them.

Simon, who was a real jock and always hungry, took one look at the spread and scooped a small mountain of potatoes onto his plate. "What happened, Mom?" he joked, "Did Dad's health food store go out of business?"

"Sorry to disappoint you, but the answer is no," Mrs. Connell said. "I just wanted to make sure you and the girls had a good meal before your Dad and I go away for the weekend. I'm leaving the refrigerator well stocked, but I don't know that I trust you kids to remember to eat right."

"Mom!" Simon protested. "I've told you a hundred times. We'll be just fine. After all, I'm seventeen years old."

"That's exactly why I'm worried." His mother smiled.

Dr. Connell set down his knife and fork reluctantly. "Kate, don't worry. The kids have promised they'll behave responsibly. Besides, the Adamses are right next door keeping an eye on things, and if any problems come up your sister Pamela lives just a few minutes away."

Sarah was concentrating on her food. She knew from experience that Simon was a lot better at handling her mom than she was.

Nicole wasn't saying anything, either. She had taken a good-sized helping of steak, but after taking one or two bites she seemed to have lost interest in eating.

Dad noticed Nicole's mood at about the same time Sarah did. "Are you feeling all right?" he asked her. "I thought you'd be hungry after your diving meet. And in good spirits, too. After all, you won another trophy for your collection."

"I feel fine," Nicole told him. "It's just that I keep thinking about my last dive. Normally, when I make a mistake I know why. But this was weird. It was almost as if I wasn't in control of my body. Something had taken over, some . . . force."

Sarah swallowed so fast she almost choked on a bite of steak. She could feel her cheeks burning. But her parents didn't notice. Their attention was focused on Nicole, and they exchanged glances.

"Don't you think you're taking this too seriously, Nicole?" Mrs. Connell suggested.

"I'm just trying to tell you how I felt," Nicole protested. "It was really weird."

Dr. Connell pushed his chair away from the table. "That settles it. You push yourself too hard, young lady. You need a rest. I think you should come up to San Francisco with us this weekend. It will get your mind off your activities for a few days, and I can keep an eye on you in case you're coming down with something."

"But Daddy, I can't! I'd miss a day of school. I'd miss cheerleading practice on Saturday! Besides, I have a date with Derek on Saturday evening."

"You can afford to miss a day of classes," Dr. Connell said. "And you can certainly afford to miss cheerleading and an evening with Derek. Your health comes first."

"*I* wouldn't mind missing a day of school," Sarah offered.

"We know that all too well." Her mother laughed. "That's why *you* can't afford to take time off. Besides, there's nothing wrong with you. You're not the one who's been having weird experiences."

That's what you think, Sarah told herself, suppressing a smile. She could never tell her mother about the strange things that had been happening to her ever since she turned thirteen. Aunt Pam was the only one who understood how tough it could be to be an apprentice witch.

Sarah helped Simon stack the dirty plates in the dishwasher and retreated to her room. Normally, she loved her bedroom. Decorated with peach-colored chintz curtains and shag rugs, and her treasured handmade patchwork quilt, the room suited her taste. But tonight she couldn't help noticing how different it was from the rest of the house, which was furnished in the sleek, uncluttered modern style her Mom and Nicole both loved.

Face it, you're a misfit, she lectured herself. You'll never get any attention in this family unless you learn to be more like Nicole.

Dejectedly, she undressed and wrapped herself in her pink terrycloth bathrobe. Maybe a long shower would help her recover her good spirits.

Out in the hall, Sarah ran into her mother.

"I've been looking for you, Nicole" her mom said. "I wanted to tell you to finish your packing tonight, because we're leaving first thing in the morning."

Mrs. Connell gave her daughter a puzzled look. "How come you're wearing your sister's bathrobe? Don't tell me yours is in the laundry. You'll need it for the trip."

"But, Mom, I'm not . . ."

The sound of her own voice made Sarah stop short. The thing was, it *wasn't* her own voice. It was Nicole's!

"Never mind," she said hurriedly. "I just borrowed this so mine will be clean for the trip. I'm taking it back right now."

To Sarah's relief, her mother shrugged her shoulders and went back downstairs.

As soon as she was gone, Sarah ran into her

room and checked herself out in the mirror. Nicole's face stared back at her. It was uncanny. She had her sister's blue eyes. Her long, straight blonde hair. Even her small, slightly turned-up nose.

Experimentally, Sarah smiled. The teeth were Nicole's too! She even had her sister's body.

Sarah paced around her room a few times, then tried doing a split. Normally, she was a little klutzy when it came to athletics. And even though she had often tried, she had never been flexible enough to do a real split. But this time, she had no trouble at all.

"This is great!" Sarah said out loud, still in Nicole's voice. "Wait till I tell Aunt Pam!"

But she couldn't very well go on being Nicole as long as her sister and her parents were still around. Mom and Dad would freak out, for one thing.

She closed her eyes and concentrated hard. "I wish I could be Sarah again until after my folks and Nicole go away," she said.

Opening her eyes, she saw her old self grinning back from the mirror.

Maybe Tina was right. Maybe she ought to try walking around in Nicole's shoes for a while. Of course, Tina had never imagined that anyone would take her advice literally. Sarah could hardly keep from laughing as she imagined how shocked Tina would be if she knew that one of her best friends was a real, live apprentice witch.

Then she thought about Nicole. She had already played one trick on her sister that day, even if it was an accident. How would Nicole feel if she knew her little sister was going around masquerading as her? She'd be furious!

"Sarah! Can I borrow your new overnight bag?" Nicole's voice interrupted Sarah's train of thought, pulling her back to reality.

"Okay," she answered. Rummaging around on the top shelf of her closet, she found the fawn-colored suitcase with genuine leather trim that her parents had given her for Christmas. She had only used the overnight bag twice, and she felt she was really being generous to lend it. But when she took it into Nicole's room, her sister didn't even bother to say thanks.

The clothes Nicole was planning to take away for the weekend were piled on her bed. Sarah recognized her handknit Irish sweater lying on top of the pile. "Hey!" she exclaimed, "that's mine. I wondered what happened to that sweater."

"You *said* I could borrow it," Nicole reminded her. "The weekend when the diving team had a training session at that resort in the mountains."

"That was two months ago!"

Nicole shrugged. "So? If you'd asked for it, I would have given it back. It slipped my mind." She shot Sarah a suspicious glance. "You don't want it back right now, do you? You won't use it this weekend anyway, and it gets really cool in San Francisco in the evenings."

"Well . . ."

"Come on," Nicole wheedled. "Don't be mean. I need it."

"Oh, all right."

Nicole picked up the sweater and folded it carefully into the large compartment of the overnight bag. Then she reached into the pile on the bed and selected a pair of cable-knit knee socks.

"Wait a second, those are mine, too," Sarah protested.

"Naturally. They go with the sweater."

"No wonder you have clothes for every occasion," Sarah shot back. "You have your wardrobe and half of mine, too. What other stuff that belongs to me have you got?"

The door of Nicole's closet was standing open. Sarah made a quick survey of the packed row of hangers and pounced on her white silk aviator's scarf, missing for at least three weeks. "I never said you could borrow this," she accused.

"Sure you did." Nicole answered. "Anyway, don't be so juvenile. You can borrow my stuff whenever you want."

"Big deal."

For some reason Sarah could never understand, Nicole and her friends dressed as if they were trying to get elected to the Preppy Hall of Fame. Nicole's closet was filled with conservative plaid skirts, tailored slacks, and oxford cloth blouses with buttons on the collars. She even wore sheer pantyhose with penny loafers.

"No wonder you're so generous," Sarah pointed out. "I wouldn't want to borrow any of your stuff."

Nicole looked bored with the whole discussion. "I wish you could take my place on this trip," she said.

"I wouldn't mind going," Sarah said a bit wistfully. We always have fun at Uncle Paul and Aunt Sylvia's."

"I know, but *I* have important things to do this weekend," Nicole said.

Sarah was getting annoyed with Nicole all over again. Her sister took it for granted that *everything* she did was important; naturally, *nothing* Sarah did could possibly matter. "You just don't want to miss your date," she teased. "What's so important about smooching with Derek?"

Nicole was too cool to be embarrassed. "If you haven't tried it, don't knock it," she said. "But I also hate to miss cheerleading practice. Coach Ramsey won't be very happy when I don't show up. Maybe you could see her and explain that Mom and Dad insisted on my going with them."

"Don't worry," Sarah promised. "I'll cover for you."

I'll do a better job of covering for you than you could possibly imagine, she added silently.

The more she thought about it, the switch seemed like a great idea. Nicole was constantly borrowing her things without asking. Why shouldn't she borrow Nicole's identity for a few hours? Maybe she could even do her sister a favor by attending cheerleading practice in her place. After all, she had learned all the cheers when Nicole was practicing for tryouts the past spring. Surely she could get through one little practice. What could possibly go wrong?

Chapter 3

For the first time she could remember, Sarah was glad that her father had a habit of making decisions at the last minute. Nicole hadn't even had time to tell her friends that she was going away.

At seven o'clock the next morning, as Mr. Connell loaded the bags into the car for the drive to the airport, Nicole rattled off a list of messages that she wanted Sarah to deliver to her friends.

"What about Derek?" Sarah asked after Nicole had already mentioned a dozen names. "Don't you have to call off your date with him?"

Nicole gave Sarah one of her aren't-you-naive looks. "Naturally, I called Derek myself. Why do you think I didn't get around to calling these other kids? By the time I finished talking to him it was too late to make any more calls."

"Naturally," Sarah echoed, giving in to the temptation to mimic her sister's voice. But Nicole was so busy thinking up more messages she didn't even notice.

Finally, the car was packed and ready. Mrs. Connell got into the back seat, and Dr. Connell sat in front with Simon, who was driving them to the airport. After long negotiations, Simon had won permission to drive the car over the weekend.

"This trip shouldn't take long," Simon told Sarah as he prepared to pull out of the driveway. "I'll be back home in time to give you a lift to school."

Sarah waved good-bye until the car disappeared around the corner of Juniper Drive, then she ran back into the house and shut herself in the upstairs bathroom. She needed every minute Simon was away to practice her transformation into Nicole.

The night before when she made the switch, it had bothered her that her bathrobe had been unchanged. She was pretty sure that wasn't the way transformations were supposed to work. If clothes weren't part of the switch, she was never going to be able to fool anyone into thinking she was Nicole.

"You can't be running around like Superman,

making quick changes in phone booths," she told her image in the mirror.

If ever she needed her aunt Pam's knowledge, this was the time, but she didn't dare ask her for help. She was sure her aunt would never approve of her trying to pass herself off as Nicole.

Instead, Sarah tried snapping her fingers and concentrating extra hard. The first three times she made the switch, she ended up looking like Nicole but still wearing her own clothes. On the fourth try, she got the clothes right, but she still had her own feet and shoes. And on the fifth try, everything changed but her ears.

"Something tells me this is going to be my weirdest experience yet," she said aloud.

She was just about to practice a sixth transformation when Simon's booming voice yelled at her through the bathroom door. "Can't you hurry up? I've been all the way to the airport and back and you're still fussing over your makeup. No one but you can see the difference anyway."

"That's what you think," Sarah muttered.

"What?" Simon shouted.

"I said, just a second," Sarah corrected herself.

Downstairs in the kitchen, she grabbed her purse and books from the table and followed Simon out to the car. For better or worse, her little experiment would soon be under way.

Dr. Connell wasn't much of a letter writer, and the note he had asked Sarah to deliver to the principal's office wasted no words. "Please excuse my daughter from today's classes," it said. "She has been feeling a little run-down lately and needs to take the day off to rest." Fortunately, her dad hadn't thought to mention which daughter was going to be out of school.

After seeing the note, Sarah had been tempted to try to take Nicole's place all day long. But a look at Nicole's schedule for the morning had changed her mind. Nicole's morning started with advanced algebra, followed by German, chemistry, and advanced placement English. She had never realized that her sister took such hard courses.

Sarah knew she could never bluff her way through any of those classes. In fact, she probably wouldn't be able to handle them even when she got to be a junior like Nicole. It would be a lot easier to wait until lunchtime and then make the switch.

Before going to homeroom, Sarah stopped at the principal's office and handed the secretary her dad's note, explaining that it was for her sister, Nicole. The secretary glanced at the message and nodded. No student would ever try to pass off such bad handwriting as a parent's.

"This seems to be in order," the secretary said, flashing a brief smile. Then to Sarah's delight, she handed back the note. Sarah pocketed it quickly. It might come in handy later on.

That morning she sat through her classes impatiently. Finally the lunch bell rang, and she managed to get out of the classroom before Micki, Tina, or her other friends could catch her and ask any inconvenient questions. On the way to the cafeteria, she ducked into the nearest girls' bathroom and locked herself into a stall. Here goes, she thought, for better or worse.

A quick snap of her fingers, and the switch was on. Opening the stall door, she cautiously checked herself out in the mirror over the sinks. For once, she seemed to have gotten all the details right. She was one hundred percent Nicole, right down to her A-line skirt, webbed belt, pin-striped blouse, and tiny, gold post earrings.

So far, so good, she told herself as she took her place in the cafeteria line. A group of Nicole's friends were seated in their usual spot at the rear of the cafeteria. As soon as she got her food, Sarah made a beeline for their table and plunked down her tray in front of an empty seat.

Before she had a chance to say a word, Nicole's best friend, Kerry Lyons, shot her a suspicious look. "What are you doing here?"

Good grief, Sarah thought. She must know I'm not Nicole. What now?

Then she remembered. Nicole was supposed to be absent. "I was feeling a little better, so I decided to come to school," she explained nervously.

Sarah's friends would have thought that was crazy. Why come to school for half a day when you already have an excuse. But Nicole's crowd was so straight-arrow that they accepted the explanation without question.

Kerry was still giving Sarah peculiar looks, though. "I can't believe you're eating that gross spaghetti," she said, pointing to Sarah's tray. "What happened to your diet? I've never seen you eat anything but salad at lunch."

"Oh, I'm just feeling hungry today," Sarah said. She hadn't realized that Nicole dieted every day. Her sister always gave the impression that she was just naturally thin.

She was still thinking over that revelation

when Jonathan Durham joined the group. Jonathan was a forward on the varsity basketball team, and even though he was no Derek, he still rated as a hunk.

Jonathan talked sports to some of the guys at the table for a few minutes. Then he turned his attention to Sarah. "How's your cute little sister?" he asked casually.

Sarah's jaw dropped almost to her knees. This was really getting interesting. She'd never dreamed that Jonathan Durham thought she was cute. "Sarah's okay," she mumbled, so surprised she could barely get the words out.

Kerry made a face. "Sarah is kind of cute, but those clothes she wears are the pits."

"They are not!" Sarah protested automatically.

"Have you lost your mind? You're always telling me how awful they are!"

"But what's wrong with what she's been wearing lately?" Sarah persisted. She knew the answer would only make her angry, but she had to know what Nicole thought about her.

"Are you kidding? How about that baggy T-shirt and denim jacket she had on the other day! You yourself said she looked like a bag lady."

"I did?" Sarah was going to say more, but

she caught herself in mid-speech. "I mean, sure I did. But I was just kidding. You know what a big kidder I am."

"What Nicole's trying to say," Jonathan put in, "is that it's okay for her to put her sister down, but she doesn't like to hear it from us. You know how loyal she is."

"Right," Sarah agreed gratefully. Her feelings toward Nicole softened a little.

"What I want to know," said a boy sitting across the table from her, "is what happened to you at the diving meet yesterday."

Sarah recognized the boy as a freestyle specialist from the boy's squad, but she couldn't think of his name. "Well, I did win the individual trophy," she reminded him.

"Sure, but we're counting on you to make it to all-state," the boy said. "And you can't do that unless you're consistent."

"But it was just one little mistake. . . ."

"One big mistake," the boy corrected her.

Whew! Sarah thought. Talk about pressure!

She had always assumed that Nicole had it easy, since she was usually the best at everything she did. Now she wasn't so sure. It must be really tough to be performing on a level where you're not expected to make *any* mistakes at all.

"The definition of consistency," the boy went

on in a lecturing tone of voice, "is that you don't make mental errors like that one. You can't afford to have lapses in concentration."

Sarah was starting to see red. "At least I won a trophy," she pointed out. "Who are you to tell me what I can't afford to do?"

To her surprise, Kerry and Jonathan burst into applause. "Way to go, Nicole," Kerry said encouragingly.

Her tormentor said nothing, and a minute or so later he picked up his tray and left the table in a huff.

"I've been waiting for someone to tell Freddy Fredericks where to get off," Jonathan said as soon as he had gone. "I just never expected it would be you."

Sarah tried to look unconcerned. Freddy Fredericks was the son of the swim coach! No wonder he had looked vaguely familiar.

She hoped she hadn't said anything that would make trouble for Nicole. But she was even more surprised to hear that her sister had a reputation for not speaking up for herself. Nicole had certainly never been shy when it came to talking back to *her*. Was it possible that she was different with her friends than she was at home?

Sarah was sorry that lunch period was just about over. She was finally starting to learn something interesting, but she had to leave soon if she wanted to change back into her own body in time for her next class.

Excusing herself from the table, she headed for the trash bin and dumped the remains of her uneaten spaghetti. She needed to be alone so she could make her switch before the class bell rang, but Kerry was right behind her, sticking to her like glue.

"I was wondering if you'd had a chance to work out your problems with Derek yet," Kerry asked in a conspiratorial tone of voice.

Sarah gulped. Problems? What problems?

"Not really," she said, stalling for time.

"Well, I think you'd better get things straightened out this weekend. What are you going to say to him?"

Sarah was starting to feel panicky. She had no idea what Kerry was talking about, and she was about to be late for class. "You know, I think I don't feel so hot," she said quickly. "Maybe I won't go to my afternoon classes after all."

Before Kerry had a chance to answer, Sarah thrust her empty tray into Kerry's hands. "Return this for me, okay?" she added. "I've got to get to the restroom."

Sarah left Kerry standing in the middle aisle of the cafeteria with a puzzled look on her face.

She felt a little bit guilty about that, but no doubt Kerry would come to the conclusion that Nicole's strange behavior was the result of her not feeling well.

As Sarah ducked into the girls' restroom just in time to change back to her own identity, she was in a slightly giddy mood. Maybe Kerry thought she had acted a little strangely, ducking out of the cafeteria like that. But no one at the lunch table had suspected that anything really strange was going on. Impersonating Nicole was turning out to be even easier than she had thought.

Not only that, but she was on the verge of finding out the inside story on Nicole and Derek. It had always bothered Sarah that Nicole didn't confide her problems to her. In fact, Nicole never admitted that she *had* any problems. Nicole always acted cool and in control, while Sarah was the flighty little sister, always rushing into situations without thinking ahead.

Kerry obviously knew better, but Sarah had been in too much of a hurry to figure out a way to get her to tell what she knew without making her suspicious. She still wasn't sure how she was going to find out what was going on with Derek. But she was sure going to try.

Chapter 4

Sarah had always envied Nicole for her part-time job at Benny's Burgers. Benny's was part of a chain of franchises, but unlike some fast-food places it had an actual kitchen where meals were cooked to order. Nicole had reported that the staff was friendly, like one big happy family, and the tips were fairly good, too. Even though Nicole only worked a few hours two afternoons a week, she made enough to keep herself in pocket money.

Better yet, Benny's was a popular hangout, not just for high school kids but for students from Oakhurst College a few miles away. The older girls at Waterview High were always scheming to meet Oakhurst guys. It seemed almost unfair that Nicole, who already had Derek, actually got paid to hang around a place where Oakhurst students dropped in every day.

Sarah didn't know the first thing about being a waitress, but she was curious to find out what it was like, so she hadn't called the restaurant to report that her sister wouldn't be coming in. Instead, she boarded a bus for the mall after school, determined to take Nicole's place for just one day. How hard could waiting tables be? she asked herself. She cleared the table at home all the time. And she certainly took orders, too, she thought with a sigh. The only difference was, she didn't get paid.

At five minutes to four, Sarah found a quiet spot in the back of Dudley's Book Nook, next door to Benny's. At four minutes to four she walked out of the bookstore, transformed into the image of her sister. Luckily, she had been in the waitresses' locker room at Benny's with Nicole and knew which of the lockers belonged to her. Luckier still, the combination to the locker was neatly penciled in a notebook Nicole carried in her backpack.

Quickly, Sarah changed into her uniform, a pink skirt and blouse topped off by a red-and-white striped apron. On her way through the kitchen she stopped to say hello to the manager, a short, thin man wearing three or four gold chains around his neck and a plastic name tag that identified him as "Mr. T". Sarah vaguely recalled that the manager's real name was Mr. Taliaferro, and the "Mr. T" was just a joke.

The restaurant itself was almost deserted. Sarah waited on a pair of women who ordered grilled cheese sandwiches and two cups of tea. When they finished eating, she delivered their check and picked up a tip. So far, the job was a snap.

Then four college guys came in and took one of the rear booths. Sarah looked them over as she arrived to take their orders. One of them was kind of cute, with green eyes and close-cropped curly hair. Not quite as cute as David Shaw, who was sort of her boyfriend, but cute.

But it was the least attractive of the four, a big, beefy, red-faced guy, who spoke up. "We'd like a round of beers," he said in a voice loud enough to be heard all the way back in the kitchen.

"I'm sorry," Sarah told him. "We don't serve beer."

"Not half as sorry as I am, Blondie," the red-faced guy said. All his friends laughed uproariously.

Some joke, Sarah thought.

"So what would you like that we're serving?"

she said, trying to keep the irritation out of her voice.

"The usual. Four cheeseburgers and four colas," came the answer.

Relieved, Sarah started to write down the order.

"Make mine with pickles and onions," the guy said.

"I'll have onions and tomatoes, but hold the pickles," said one of his friends.

"I'll have the same," said another. "No, on second thought, hold the onions but give me a side of cole slaw."

"Sounds good," said the fourth. "But hold the cole slaw, and give me pickles and a side of French fries."

The first guy chimed in again. "I'll have fries, too. And cole slaw. But forget the pickles and give me two slices of tomato."

That set off another round of changes, with Sarah madly trying to write fast enough to keep the orders straight. She knew the guys were purposely giving her a hard time, but she wasn't sure how to handle the situation. If she told them off and got into trouble for it, Nicole was the one who would suffer.

Finally, the guys got tired of fooling around, and she was able to deliver their orders to the kitchen. When she returned, a mother and two little girls were sitting at one of her tables. "I'll have a chocolate milk shake," the older girl said. "Me, too," her sister chimed in.

Sarah's heart sank. It was her job to fill the beverage orders, and she had no idea how to mix a milk shake. Going behind the counter she grabbed two metal shake containers and poured some milk into each of them. Obviously a milk shake must have milk in it. But what else? After some thought, she added a squirt of chocolate syrup. The next ingredient had to be ice cream, which was stored in big tubs in the freezers under the counter. When she finally located the tub of chocolate, it was so hard that it took her several minutes and all her strength to dig out several generous scoops.

By the time she finished, the little girls were looking very impatient. She also noticed that two more of her tables had filled up with customers, and the college guys' cheeseburgers had appeared in the serving window that connected the counter area and the kitchen.

Hurriedly she attached the milk shake containers to the gleaming chrome mixing machine. She had no idea how long it took to mix a shake, so she decided to leave the machine on a good long time just to make sure. While she was waiting for the shakes, she decided to deliver the cheeseburgers.

Balancing a tray filled with burgers, cole slaw, fries, and four tall glasses of cola, she staggered over to the boys' booth and unloaded all the food. The red-faced guy lifted a corner of his cheeseburger bun and frowned. "We wanted rare cheeseburgers, Blondie. These are well done."

"You never said anything about wanting your burgers rare," Sarah protested.

The red-faced boy shrugged. "Look honey, we're in here every week. And we always want our burgers rare. You ought to know that by now. So what's the big deal?"

Sarah sighed. She wasn't sure if he was telling the truth or not, but it looked as if she had no choice but to take all four cheeseburgers back to the kitchen. She was just loading them onto her tray when there was a loud crash behind the counter, and the two little girls at the front table started screaming.

Sarah wheeled around to see what had happened, and her heart sank. She must not have fastened the milk shake containers onto the machine correctly, because one of them had come loose. The can had rocketed off the mixing machine and landed on the floor, leaving a shower of chocolately goo everywhere — on the floor, the counter top, and the formerly gleaming mirror attached to the wall behind the counter.

Naturally the college guys thought the scene was hilarious.

The mother of the little girls was not laughing, however. "My daughters have their hearts set on a shake," she announced. "But they want to drink it, not wear it."

Sarah raced to the counter and started mopping up the mess, hoping to clean up the worst of the goo before Mr. T showed up to find out what the noise was about. All the customers were angry over having to wait so long for their food, and two more parties of college kids had just arrived, making four tables that hadn't even ordered yet.

Worst of all, Sarah felt strange, sort of tingly all over. Her feet were aching, too, and her shoes suddenly felt a size too small. It was almost as if her feet were growing, changing back from Nicole's petite six-and-a-halfs, to Sarah's own size eights. And as she scrubbed the counter frantically to get rid of the last traces of spilled shake, she noticed that her hands were changing too. Nicole's neatly manicured nails, done with just a touch of clear polish, were gone, replaced by her own pearly pink ones.

This is *weird*, Sarah thought. I'm turning back into myself piece by piece. But why? And what can I do about it? The customers were sure to notice soon, and when they did they would freak out.

Just then Mr. T came out of the kitchen. "Nicole! *What* are you doing? The place is a mess! No one's served! We can't have you just idling around doing nothing while the customers wait for their meals."

"Doing nothing!" Sarah cried. "I'm working as hard as I can. It's just that I can't keep up."

Sarah realized immediately that this was the wrong thing to say. Mr. T was frowning. "If that's really the case, then I'll be forced to let you go," he said.

That was all she needed! Nicole would never understand if she came back from her weekend and found that she'd been fired from the job she loved. She'd think Mr. T had lost his mind, and Sarah would feel guilty for the rest of her life.

"Please, Mr. T," she pleaded. "I'll do better next week. I don't know what's wrong with me today."

At least that last part was true, Sarah thought ruefully.

"All right," the manager relented. "No use crying over spilled milkshakes. Now let's take care of these customers."

Mr. T went over to serve the groups that hadn't ordered yet, and Sarah took the college guys their cheeseburgers. This time, they were rare as ordered, but her tormentors were not ready to leave her alone. Examining his burger intently, the red-faced boy pretended to find a hair in his food. "What's this?" he demanded in mock indignation, pointing at an object invisible to everyone but himself. "I can't eat this, Blondie. Take it back."

Sarah was fed up. "Number one, my name is not Blondie. And number two, there's nothing wrong with that cheeseburger, so stop playing with your food and grow up."

The rest of the group broke into loud guffaws, and the boy's red face got even redder, aware that this time his friends were laughing at him, not with him. Getting up from the booth, he confronted the manager. "Your waitress just insulted me," he whined.

Sarah's heart sank. Now she was going to be fired for sure.

Mr. T was more than a foot shorter than the angry college student, but he wasn't the least bit intimidated. "You should be ashamed of yourself," he said calmly. "Now sit down and behave."

To Sarah's shock, the boy's mood changed

immediately. "Yes, sir," he said, meekly heading back to his booth.

"You should have talked back to that big bully a long time ago," Mr. T said a few minutes later, after he'd delivered the customers' orders to the kitchen. "I've noticed him giving you a hard time for a few weeks now, and I was wondering how much you'd put up with."

The manager examined her with a look of kindly concern. "Are you all right? Somehow you look different today. . . ."

Glancing up at her image in the mirror behind the counter, Sarah jumped. A minute or two ago her eyes had been china blue, just like Nicole's. Now she saw her own brown eyes staring back at her. The combination of Nicole's features and her own eyes was really spooky.

"I guess I'm just tired," she said lamely.

Mr. T smiled. "Tell you what. Everything's under control here. Why don't you knock off early?"

Sarah was so glad to have an excuse to leave that she practically hugged Mr. T. Racing into the staff room, she changed in record time, and seconds later she sprinted across the parking lot and jumped aboard the town bus just as it was about to depart.

Her illusions about college men were certainly shattered! She had imagined that any guy old enough and rich enough to be a student at Oakhurst would be smooth and sophisticated, but now she knew better. No doubt there were some nice Oakhurst students, but the group she'd just met were A-one jerks.

And as for Nicole's dream job, she could have it! She had never realized it before, but apparently there were a few people around who thought it was really amusing to pick on waitresses, especially when they were young and inexperienced.

Sarah hoped that by the time she was old enough to have a part-time job she'd be able to handle the hassles. And in the meantime she had a new respect for Nicole. Her life wasn't as easy as she'd thought.

Chapter 5

Sarah had been so relieved to get away from Benny's that she hadn't bothered to think about how she looked. But now, as the bus made its way down Main Street toward her own neighborhood, she was starting to feel nervous. Simon might be home when she arrived, so she'd have to make sure she was herself again before she got home. At least for the moment though, she was safe.

Or was she?

No sooner had she let herself relax than she heard a very familiar voice calling out from the rear of the bus.

"Nicole! What are you doing here? I thought you were away for the weekend."

Micki Davis, Sarah's best friend in the whole world, came lurching her way from the back of the bus and dropped into the seat behind her.

"Uh . . ." Sarah's mind was a complete blank. It wasn't easy to lie to your best friend under any circumstances, and at the moment she couldn't think of a single excuse to explain how Nicole could be riding the Main Street bus when she was also in San Francisco.

Anyway, Micki wasn't waiting for an answer. She was carefully studying her friend's eyes. "How come your eyes are brown?" she asked. "What did you do, get tinted contacts?"

"That's right. They're tinted contacts," Sarah lied, latching onto the suggestion gratefully. But the voice that came out of her mouth sounded more like her own than Nicole's. The spell that had turned her into her sister was definitely wearing off.

Micki wasn't fooled for long. "Sarah, is that you?" she asked accusingly.

Sarah nodded. "But don't tell anyone what I'm doing," she said in a low voice. "Nicole would never forgive me."

Micki sucked in her breath. "It would be hard to blame her. How come you're doing this?"

"To tell you the truth, I'm not even sure any more," Sarah admitted. "I guess I was just curious. Everything always comes so easy to Nicole. She's the smart one. The athletic one. The cute blonde who just has to bat her eyelashes to get her way. And her life has always been more exciting than mine."

"Until recently," Micki pointed out.

That was true. Nicole might have a lot of advantages, but she didn't have Sarah's supernatural powers. Sarah felt a little thrill of triumph. For the first time in her life, she had a talent that her sister couldn't compete with.

But the feeling of satisfaction didn't last long. "The trouble is," she wailed, "no one knows I'm a witch. Except for you and Aunt Pam, I mean. So what good does it do? As far as the world is concerned I'm still Nicole Connell's scatter-brained kid sister."

"It's what *you* know that counts," Micki reminded her.

"Maybe you're right," Sarah conceded. "But where's the fun in that? Besides, so far almost nothing I've tried to do with my powers has worked out. And look at me now! I can't even control the way I look."

Micki giggled. "You do look awfully silly."

"Thanks a lot."

"But you *can* go back to being yourself, can't you?" Micki asked anxiously. "You've got to manage in time for tonight."

"Why? What's tonight?"

"Don't you remember?" Micki asked, her

brown eyes widening with exasperation. "We're supposed to go to the movies with Rick and David."

Sarah looked dumbfounded.

"David," Micki repeated. "David Shaw. Your boyfriend. Remember him?"

"Uh, yeah. Sure." But Sarah had to admit that she'd scarcely given David a thought since this business with Nicole started. She'd waved hello to him a few times as she rushed past him in the halls at school, but that was about it.

Now that Micki had reminded her though, she realized that this was one date she couldn't get out of. David's job throwing pizzas at the Pizza Palace kept him busy most weeknights and part of the weekend. Usually he had Saturday nights off and worked Fridays. But this week he had switched with a friend who had to attend a wedding, so tonight was their only chance to go out all weekend.

"What am I going to do?" Sarah wailed. "I can't stand David up tonight. He'd be really upset. But I can't let him see me like this, either!"

"I don't know," Micki warned, "but you have exactly one hour to get your act together. David is no dummy. He'll know right away that something weird is going on. Besides, I really need your support tonight. I'm nervous enough about going out with Rick. He's so cute. I'll probably get all tongue-tied and make a complete fool of myself."

"No, you won't," Sarah reassured her. "It'll be just fine."

Sarah wasn't as sure as she sounded, but she decided to keep her thoughts to herself. Rick was a private school student whom Micki had met one day while shopping at the mall. According to Micki he was really cute. But that could be part of the problem. Micki claimed that what she really wanted in a boyfriend was someone warm, sensitive, smart, and funny — a lot like their buddy Matt Neville, in fact. But that didn't stop her from getting crushes on guys who were just the opposite of what she said she wanted.

"Are you sure you wouldn't rather go out with Rick alone?" Sarah suggested hopefully. "I mean, a double date isn't exactly the best opportunity to get to know someone. Maybe you'd rather have him to yourself all evening."

Micki shook her head vigorously. "No way. I'd probably be paralyzed with fright. I need you guys around. You're sort of my safety net. Besides, if Rick sees that you two are my friends, he'll know I'm not a complete doofus, no matter how much I mess up."

* * *

So Sarah had no choice. Unless she wanted to have both her boyfriend and her best friend mad at her, she had to work out her problem, and do it fast.

Sarah closed her eyes and concentrated hard, willing herself to change back into good, old, one hundred percent Sarah. But for some reason she didn't understand, the spell wouldn't work. She was starting to get really scared now.

There was only one solution. She would have to go to her aunt Pamela for advice. She hated to do that, because she was pretty sure that her aunt would disapprove of her trying to switch places with Nicole.

But the situation was rapidly becoming an emergency. Looking at her reflection in the bus window, Sarah saw a face that seemed to be split down the middle — the right half of her face looked like herself, the left half like her sister. Even her hair was affected, straight and wispy blonde on one side, thick and dark on the other.

Micki thought her predicament was funny.

"Talk about split personalities!" Micki said, laughing so hard there were tears in her eyes. "You've really got it bad."

"Some friend you are!" Sarah shot back. "This is the worst thing that's ever happened to me!"

Micki wiped her eyes. "I'm sorry, I just can't help it."

The bus was making its way through the quiet streets of the village, the boutique-lined shopping district where Aunt Pamela's store was located. Sarah knew she couldn't go home the way she was. Her only chance was to make a break for it, and hope her aunt was still at the store.

"Here, let me borrow your scarf," she said.

Micki untied the blue silk scarf that she was wearing as a belt and Sarah quickly used it to cover her hair. "I'm getting off here. See you in an hour."

She waited until the bus had already opened its doors for the Lynne Street stop. Then, hunching over to hide her face from the other passengers, she bolted down the aisle, hopped off, and ran all the way to her aunt's door.

Five minutes later, Sarah found herself sitting in the back room of Aunt Pam's shop, sipping a soothing cup of tea.

Aunt Pam's store was a combination teashop and bookstore. Sarah liked everything about it, starting with the name: Plates and Pages. Aunt Pam had decorated the shop herself, using lots of wicker chairs, delicate leafy ferns, and exotic-looking flowering plants. But the best thing about the shop was the pungent aroma of the herbs and spices her aunt sold as a sideline. Ever since Sarah could remember, Aunt Pam's store had always made her feel calm and serene, as if the problems of the everyday world were a million miles away. And that was one spell that still seemed to be working for her.

When Sarah arrived at the shop, Aunt Pam was waiting on her last customer of the day, and she had curtly motioned for Sarah to wait in the back room until she closed up. Sarah had expected a lecture. Instead, Aunt Pam studied her strange appearance and shook her head sadly, more worried than angry.

"This is partly my fault," she announced. "I should have known this might happen. Envy is a powerful emotion, especially between sisters. The same thing happened to me when I was an apprentice witch. I couldn't resist trying out Kate's life. It seemed so much more exciting than mine."

"Really?" Sarah was amazed. "I mean, not that my mom isn't beautiful and everything. It's just hard to imagine you ever wanting to be anyone but yourself."

Aunt Pam smiled. She was wearing one of her typical outfits, a rose-colored leotard matched with a long, swirling skirt, topped off by a magnificent antique silk shawl in a rich pattern of rose, gold, and silver. A half dozen simple gold bracelets emphasized the slenderness of her wrists and her beautifully manicured hands. And her long, black hair was gathered into a single, thick braid that hung nearly to her waist.

Most people couldn't get away with dressing like that, Sarah thought. But on Aunt Pam, these exotic styles look just right.

"Finding out who you are is part of growing up," Aunt Pam said. "And part of that is trying out different styles. It's natural, even though sometimes it leads to making mistakes."

"Well, I've learned my lesson," Sarah agreed. "Just help me get back to being myself, and this is one mistake I'll never make again."

Her aunt's smile faded. "I'm afraid it's not that easy. One thing you have to learn, Sarah, is that there are some spells you can't just turn on and off at will. Once you've set them in motion, you have to see them through to the end."

"Huh? You mean you can't make me look like me again?"

"Not for good. You won't get rid of this spell until you've learned to get inside Nicole's head. It isn't enough to look like her. You've got to see the world through her eyes."

"But I can't go around looking like this!"

Sarah protested. "What will people think?"

Aunt Pam poured her another cup of tea from her flowered porcelain teapot. "It isn't that bad, fortunately. I can show you how to control your appearance in the short run."

After rummaging in one of the drawers of her desk, her aunt returned with a perfume vial labeled *Transformation*. "Rub a dab of this behind your left ear when you want to make the switch," she instructed Sarah. "But be careful. This potion wears off after an hour, and this is the last of my supply. So use it sparingly."

Gratefully, Sarah hugged her. "You're a lifesaver, Aunt Pam. I'm not sure I understand what you mean about getting inside Nicole's head, but I'll do my best."

For the moment all Sarah wanted was to go back to being herself. Cautiously she dabbed on a tiny drop of her aunt's potion, and watched with relief as her looks returned to normal.

She'd been pretty scared on the bus. But in spite of what her aunt had said, she found it hard to imagine that she would keep assuming Nicole's identity again, even when she didn't want it. Still, she decided that she'd better tuck the vial into her purse, just to be safe. If the spell really wasn't broken, she just might need its help again before the weekend was over.

Chapter 6

"I'd like you to meet Rick," Micki said as Sarah popped into the back seat of the Davis's car later that evening.

Micki's mom, Mrs. Davis, was driving them to the movie theater, and Micki and Rick were sitting next to her in the front seat. He turned and flashed Sarah an impish grin.

Sarah smiled back. But she was thinking that there was something about Rick that looked strangely familiar. Was it his green eyes? His short, curly hair?

Just as they stopped to pick up David, Sarah suddenly had an inspiration. "You don't happen to have a brother who goes to Oakhurst College, do you?" she asked.

"Sure do," Rick said proudly. "He's the manager of the football team. Do you know him?"

Sarah felt sure that Rick's brother was one

of the kids who had given her such a hard time in Benny's. But of course, she couldn't admit to meeting him there. "I don't really know him," she said, thinking fast. "But I guess my brother Simon may have mentioned him."

Micki turned around and gave Sarah a quizzical look. She knew very well that Simon didn't know Rick's brother.

Sarah, meanwhile, was tempted to take Micki aside at the first opportunity and warn her about this guy. But then, maybe she was being too hasty. Rick couldn't help what his brother was like. And maybe he would turn out to be perfectly nice himself.

Unfortunately, he didn't get off to a very good start. No sooner had David jogged down the driveway and ducked into the back seat next to Sarah, than an argument started over what movie to see. Sarah and David were both in favor of catching the new Michael J. Fox comedy that was playing. Rick wanted to go to *Damon the Destroyer*, a sword-and-sorcery epic that was featured in one of the other theaters at Cinema Six.

"I saw the first in that series, *Damon the Dagger-Thrower*, and the special effects were really cheap," David complained. "Strictly amateur night. The tyrannosaurus that Damon fought looked like something that came out of a cereal box. I mean, you could actually see the seams in the plastic. When it fell over, I kept expecting this huge hand to swoop down and set it back on its feet."

Sarah laughed, but Rick wasn't about to give in easily. "But I already saw the comedy," he argued. "I don't want to see it twice."

"Well then, we can't make you see it twice," Micki spoke up. "I vote for *Damon*."

Sarah didn't need her second sight to know that Rick was lying. The comedy had just opened a few days before, for one thing. But for Micki's sake she decided not to challenge Rick. She was glad just to be Sarah again. After her hectic day, it seemed petty to argue over which movie to see.

When they got to Cinema Six, they learned that *Damon the Destroyer* wasn't going to start for another twenty-five minutes. David ambled off in the direction of the refreshments counter, and the others settled down in an empty corner of the lobby. A few minutes later David returned carrying a tub of popcorn big enough to feed an elephant.

"Didn't you eat any dinner?" Micki teased, following up her comment by helping herself to a big handful of popcorn.

While the others munched away, Sarah's attention was riveted on the door, where five junior boys were just lining up to buy tickets for the Michael J. Fox movie. Derek Crawford was in the middle of the group, dressed in a turquoise-and-white rugby shirt that emphasized his muscular chest and shoulders.

Sarah had always thought Derek was more than okay looking, but tonight her reaction was different. Just the sight of him standing there, absent-mindedly running his fingers through his hair as he talked to his friends, made her heart beat faster.

She tried reminding herself that this was the same Derek she resented for treating her like a little kid — and the same Derek who, despite his good looks, had about as much personality as a macaroni salad. But it was hopeless. She had fallen instantly, wildly in love with her sister's boyfriend.

Sarah had no idea why this was happening. All she knew was that at that moment she desperately wanted to be with Derek.

"Excuse me," she told David and the others. "I'm going to the ladies' room."

"Wait, I'll come with you," Micki offered.

"No, that's okay. I've got to make a phone call, too. I forgot to give Simon a message." It was a lame excuse, but David and Micki accepted it, and Sarah hurried off before Micki could change her mind.

Ducking into one of the phone booths that lined the alcove around the corner, Sarah reached into her purse and fished out the tiny crystal vial marked *Transformation*. She had promised herself she wasn't going to use this stuff, but this was an emergency, and the liquid in the bottle was more effective than trying to wish to be Nicole.

Here goes, she thought, dabbing a tiny dot of the oil behind her left ear.

After counting slowly to five, she opened her eyes and checked her appearance in her compact mirror. This stuff really works, she exulted. She looked exactly like Nicole, and on the first try, too!

Luckily, David, Micki, and Rick were so busy eating that they didn't even notice her scurrying back across the lobby. Latching on to Derek's elbow, she pulled him back into a quiet corner behind the refreshment stand.

"Hey-uh, Nicole!" he said, looking pleased at her surprise appearance. "What's up? I thought you were away for the weekend. Then some of the kids said they saw you in the lunchroom today."

"The folks changed their plans again," Sarah told him. "You know how parents are."

"This time, it's fine with me." Derek flashed a smile that made Sarah weak in the knees. "I guess we're going to see the same film," he added. "Let's sit together."

"I'm afraid I can't. I'm here to see *Damon the Destroyer*." Sarah searched her mind for an explanation. "I don't have a choice because I'm here with my sister and her friends, and I promised I'd stay with them tonight."

"Baby-sitting, huh?" Derek smiled indulgently.

Sarah all but bit her tongue. Normally, she'd be livid at the mere thought that she and David needed a baby-sitter. But tonight, Derek could do and say no wrong. "That's more or less it," she said. "Anyway, they're all determined to see *Damon the Destroyer*."

Derek laughed. "Your kid sister would want to see that movie. She really is immature for her age."

"I — " Sarah caught herself in time. "I mean, *she* is not!"

Derek shrugged. "I know you always defend her. . . ."

"I do?" It was hard to believe that Nicole stuck up for her. At home she was constantly criticizing every little thing Sarah did.

Derek looked mildly annoyed. "Sure you do. Why deny it? But for just this once, I kind of agree with her. Even though the movie is junk, it's the kind of junk I like."

Was she just imagining it? Sarah wondered. Or was Derek getting smarter? He was starting to sound almost witty.

But Derek was still slowly working out the implications of Nicole being at home for the weekend. "How about tomorrow night?" Derek wanted to know. "Does this mean we're still on for the dance?"

"Sure thing." The way she felt at this moment, Sarah wouldn't have dreamed of turning down a chance to spend a whole Saturday evening with Derek. Going to a dance with him would be too much!

"Good," he said. He put his arm around Sarah's shoulders and gave her a quick hug.

Sarah felt herself practically melting. Was this how Nicole felt with Derek? She had always wondered why her smart sister was attracted to someone like him, but now she was starting to understand.

"After the dance, maybe we can finish the talk we started the other day." Derek said. "Have you made up your mind yet?"

"My mind?" Sarah echoed stupidly.

She had no idea what Derek was talking about. If only she had managed to think of a way to get Kerry to tell her just what Nicole's problem with Derek was!

"I guess I need more time," she stalled.

Derek frowned. "Right. But remember, you promised to make up your mind this weekend."

Whatever the problem was, she didn't want to think about it now. All she wanted was to be with Derek.

Unfortunately, the movie he had come to see was starting. His friends had already gotten tired of waiting and gone inside the theater.

"Look, I gotta go," Derek said finally.

Sarah thought fast. "Maybe I can get away from my sister and her friends after all. I could come sit with you."

"Sure." Derek shrugged. "We'll be in our usual spot. Right down front."

Derek disappeared into the theater. And Sarah, after making sure she was alone, dabbed a droplet of *Transformation* behind her ear and hurried back to her friends in the lobby. When she rejoined them, Rick was in the middle of recounting the plot of the first *Damon* movie.

"I really loved the part where Damon attacks the dragon with his laser sword. What a battle! SWACK! POW! KA-BAM!"

Micki made a face. Rick might be cute, but he was turning out to be a little nerdy.

Rick noticed Micki's funny expression, but misunderstood the cause. "Sorry," he apologized, "I guess you girls don't like violence."

"I love violence," Micki disagreed. "I even watch wrestling on TV. I watch old horror movies, too. What I can't stand is hearing someone re-tell the entire plot of a movie I've already seen."

"Well *excuse* me." Rick said with a huff, trying to make a joke of Micki's put-down.

Suddenly Sarah felt sorry for him. She had made up her mind not to like Rick because of his brother, but maybe she'd been too hasty. He couldn't help what his brother was like. Besides, Micki and David could be a tough audience. They knew each other so well, and were always cracking private jokes. No wonder Rick was a little nervous.

"Personally, I liked Rick's version better than the movie," she said.

Rick shot her a grateful look. "If you really want to see the other movie, we could," he offered. "We've only missed a few minutes of it."

Micki and David were ready to take him up on the offer. But Sarah shook her head. If she ended up in the same theater with Derek and his friends it would be a disaster.

When it was time for them to go into the theater, she steered the group toward four seats in the back row. Sarah was careful to drop back so that she got the aisle seat, with David next to her and Micki and Rick on the other side of him.

The lights went down and the music started. On the screen, Damon, dressed in a leopard-skin loin cloth, was battling his way out of a dungeon infested with rats as big as trailer trucks. Rick and Micki were engrossed in the picture. And even David, for all he pretended not to like movies like this, was watching intently, his face frozen in an expression of horrified amusement.

Here's my chance, Sarah thought.

Leaning over, she whispered in David's ear. "I'm going to the ladies' room. Be right back."

Without taking his eyes off the screen, David nodded.

Sarah slipped out of her seat and tiptoed up the aisle. In the deserted hallway outside, she pulled out the vial of magic liquid and changed herself back into Nicole.

Seconds later, she ducked into the adjoining theater and made her way down to the front row. Sure enough, Derek had saved her a place. Ignoring the whistles and cries of "Down in front" from the spectators behind her, she crawled over the knees of the people sitting nearest the aisle and sank into the empty seat.

Derek automatically reached over and covered her hand with his much larger one. Sarah was in heaven. Here she was, a mere freshman, holding hands with a junior — and not just any junior, either! Half the girls in school were swooning over Derek.

If only Micki could see this, Sarah thought, she would probably die of envy!

Sarah just wished that she hadn't thought of that word — envy. Unfortunately, it reminded her of what Aunt Pam had said about her weekend project. Was she only taking Nicole's place out of jealousy? Or was her desire to live her sister's life just normal, healthy curiosity?

Instead of concentrating on the experience of holding hands with Derek, Sarah found herself debating the rights and wrongs of what she was doing. On the one hand, she didn't mean any harm, she assured herself. On the other hand, Nicole would no doubt be really steamed if she knew that her little sister was out with her boyfriend.

Sarah felt guilty. But not quite guilty enough to stop what she was doing. She stayed in her seat for at least half an hour, pretending to watch the show. Only the thought that David and the others must be wondering what happened to her forced her to decide to go back to the other theater.

Giving Derek's hand a playful squeeze, she whispered, "Got to go. See you tomorrow night, okay?"

Derek leaned over and kissed her.

It was just a peck on the cheek, an almost absentminded good-bye kiss. But Sarah was elated. I'll never wash that spot again, she promised herself.

Out in the hall, she made the switch back into her own body, then returned to the theater where her friends were watching *Damon the Destroyer*. Damon must have conquered the giant rats, because he was now riding through the jungle on the back of an elephant. Sitting behind him on the same elephant was a sun-tanned woman with a punk haircut, who was dressed in what looked like a bathing suit made of python skin.

"Who's that?" Sarah whispered.

"Snake Woman," David hissed back. From the way he said it, it was hard to tell whether he meant the woman on the screen or Sarah.

Obviously David had noticed how long she'd been gone, and he didn't seem any too pleased.

The movie ended with Damon and Snake Woman doing battle with an army of monkey-people from the planet Chimpeter.

As the lights went up, David snorted derisively. "Did those monkey-aliens remind you of anything? To me they looked just like the flying monkeys in the *The Wizard of Oz*! I bet they even recycled the same costumes."

Sarah breathed a sigh of relief. At least David wasn't going to start interrogating her right away. Instead he was discussing the movie with Rick. That was typical of David. He hated films like this, or so he said, but he had watched it so intently that he could debate the fine points of the production with Siskel and Ebert.

After the movie they walked around for a while and then stopped for sodas at a place nearby. Everything was fine until they returned to the place where they were supposed to wait for Mrs. Davis to pick them up. Micki and Rick were having an awkward conversation comparing public and private schools, when David steered Sarah around the corner for a private talk.

"What's going on?" he demanded.

Sarah regarded him with what she hoped would pass for a look of wide-eyed innocence. "Nothing," she lied.

"That's not good enough," David told her. "If you have some kind of problem, you can tell me what it is. I'll help you if I can. But don't try to tell me that nothing's going on."

Suddenly, Sarah was struck by a funny

thought. First Derek had wanted to talk over some kind of problem that he was having with Nicole. Now David was insisting that she, Sarah, had a problem. She had always thought that girls were supposed to be the serious ones while guys hated these soul-baring discussions. That certainly wasn't true of these two — especially David!

She'd had fun tonight, and she hadn't done or said anything that could hurt anyone. And now David was trying to make a federal case out of it.

"Lighten up, David," she cajoled. "Just because I was gone for a few minutes, there's no reason to get all upset."

"A few minutes! You hardly said a word to me all evening! I hardly even saw you!"

"Okay, I'm sorry. . . . What more do you want?"

David shrugged. "I guess I want a girlfriend who's honest with me — not playing some kind of game that I don't even know the rules to."

Sarah knew this was no time for laughing and fooling around. David didn't talk this way very often, but when he did he meant every word he said. Unfortunately she was in a giddy mood.

"Games?" she giggled. "You mean like baseball? Or tiddlywinks?"

"I give up," David said. "I'm going home alone."

David went over to the phone booth on the corner and called his brother. By the time Mrs. Davis arrived, David's brother had already come by to pick him up.

Micki seemed more worried about the fight than about her own date with Rick. "Are you okay?" she asked Sarah. "Don't worry. I'm sure you'll make up soon."

Sarah was already bored with the subject. "David's making a big deal out of nothing," she said with a laugh. "I had a good time tonight, and I'm not going to let him ruin it."

For the rest of the trip home, Sarah chatted with Rick about the movie. Micki didn't seem to have much to say. Sarah assumed that was because her date with Rick hadn't worked out all that well.

At least she had enjoyed herself, even if the others hadn't. The best part about it was that Derek had been completely fooled. With the help of the potion she'd gotten from Aunt Pam, the whole business of changing identities had become ridiculously easy.

Chapter 7

When they arrived at Rick's house, Micki got out for a few minutes to say good-bye, while Mrs. Davis and Sarah sat in the car. Judging by the expression on Micki's face, it wasn't exactly a warm farewell. Sarah guessed that Rick and Micki wouldn't be having a second date. Not that that would be any great loss! Rick was borderline nerdy, in Sarah's judgment. Not exactly hopeless, but not worth losing any sleep over, either.

On the other hand, she couldn't wait to tell Micki about what had happened with Derek. When Rick had disappeared inside his front door and Micki returned to the car, Sarah jumped into the backseat next to her friend.

"I talked to Derek!" she whispered excitedly. "I even sat next to him. It was great! I think I'm in love!"

"Good for you," Micki said. But her sarcastic tone of voice suggested she couldn't care less.

"Don't you want to hear the details?" Sarah persisted. "It was wild. He didn't suspect a thing."

Micki turned to face her friend. "No, I don't want to hear the details. Furthermore, I think you're incredibly self-centered!"

Sarah was shocked. Micki was so steady, so cheerful. It wasn't like her to show anger, especially at Sarah. Unlike many best friends, the two of them rarely argued.

"I don't get it," Sarah said. "What did I do? I thought you were on my side. Don't you want to hear how I got along as Nicole?"

Micki shot Sarah a warning look and motioned in the direction of her mother. Mrs. Davis was studiously keeping her eyes on the road, apparently paying no attention to the conversation in the back seat. But Sarah still couldn't afford to risk talking about her life as a witch in front of an adult.

Micki waited until they pulled up in front of Sarah's. And while her mom waited patiently in the car once again, she followed her friend to the door of the Connell house.

"I just think you were really selfish tonight," Micki announced. "You left David alone all evening. And me, too. I told you I needed moral support. Rick thought you kept ducking out because you hated him. Then on the ride home, you talked constantly. We didn't have a chance to say a word to each other."

"Micki, I'm sorry. But I was so excited about being Nicole. I mean, this is a major event! How many girls can transform themselves into their own sisters! Besides, now I'm starting to think that I'm in love with Derek. . . ."

There, she said it out loud. Of all the things she had envied about Nicole's life, Derek had been last on the list. But tonight she had felt so attracted to him. Did she have the nerve to try to steal her own sister's boyfriend? That would be about as low as you could get, she told herself. Besides, she doubted that she could do it even if she wanted to.

Sarah's train of thought was broken by Mrs. Davis, who had finally run out of patience. Rolling down the car window, she called out in an exasperated tone of voice, "Girls, please . . . you talk to each other all day. Can't this wait?"

"I might as well leave," Micki said coldly. "You weren't paying a bit of attention to what I was saying anyway. Call me if you decide you're willing to listen to what *I* have to say."

That was almost exactly what David had told her, Sarah thought as she watched the Davis's car pull away. Since both of them were angry with her, she must be partly at fault. Still, she couldn't help feeling that neither of them were being very understanding.

She felt that way especially about Micki. After all, Micki knew her secret. She had even been part of her last adventure, traveling in time all the way back to the 1860's. So why was she making such a big deal about a simple evening at the movies?

I'll worry about that tomorrow, Sarah told herself. Tomorrow is another day.

That was Scarlett O'Hara's line from *Gone With the Wind*, of course. But it was amazing how often it came in handy since this witch business had started. She could always patch things up with David and Micki. Right now she had to make up her mind what she was going to do about Derek.

When Sarah let herself inside the house, she found her brother in the kitchen, fixing himself a sandwich of leftover sliced steak and onions.

The sight of all that mouth-watering food made Sarah realize that she hadn't eaten all day. She'd left the food untouched at lunch, because she didn't want to make Kerry suspicious. And for the rest of the day her schedule had been so busy that she hadn't had a chance to eat anything. How did Nicole do it? Maybe she just skipped meals because she didn't have time.

The thought made Sarah shudder. She loved to eat, and it wasn't often that she missed a meal.

"Don't put that stuff away," she told Simon, motioning in the direction of the sandwich making. She grabbed a knife and started slicing an onion while Simon split an extra roll and put it in the toaster oven for her.

"What would David say if he saw you eating that much onion?" he teased.

"Nothing," Sarah said with a shrug. "We had a fight. He'll probably never speak to me again."

Simon whistled softy. "What about?"

"It's hard to say, really. David was just being a sour puss."

"That's funny. I always thought David was pretty sensible. Compared to Derek, he's practically a genius."

Now that she was at home and the spell of the evening had been broken by her tiff with Micki, Sarah was no longer quite so sure she was in love with Derek. Maybe she had let herself get carried away by the excitement of the moment. Still, she bristled at hearing her brother make fun of him. "There's nothing wrong with Derek," she declared firmly. "He's a lot smarter than other people think."

Simon took his finished sandwich and sat down at the table. "I'm sorry you feel that way. I thought Derek was one subject we agreed on wholeheartedly. I mean, not even Nicole ever claimed Derek was intelligent. She just goes out with him because he's the boy all the popular girls in her class want."

"That isn't fair to Nicole," Sarah said. "Besides, you don't know Derek, or you wouldn't put him down like that."

"I know him as well as you do."

"No, you don't," she shot back.

Simon raised his eyebrows. "Since when do you know Derek so well?"

Too late, Sarah realized that she had said too much. When will I ever learn to keep my big mouth shut? she wondered.

She took a big bite of her sandwich and started chewing vigorously, hoping that Simon would let the subject drop. But he was obviously intrigued. "If you've been busy learning to appreciate muscleman Derek, it's no wonder David is upset," he mused.

Experience had taught Sarah that her brother was an expert at worming the truth out of her. The best way to deal with him when he wanted to know something was to clam up.

"Why do you think the folks insisted on Nicole going with them this weekend?" she asked, changing the subject. "Nicole may be a little run-down, but keeping her out of school for a day was a drastic solution, don't you think?"

Simon grinned. Obviously he had some theories of his own on this subject. "If you ask me, I think Mom and Dad just lost their nerve."

"Lost their nerve? What do you mean?"

"Look at it this way," Simon explained. "Mom and Dad don't worry so much about me because I'm a boy. And they don't worry about you all that much either because, well, you're the baby of the family. But Nicole is a different story. I bet they got cold feet when it came to leaving her unsupervised for a whole weekend."

Sarah felt a wave of indignation. "I can get in just as much trouble as Nicole can!" It wasn't exactly something to be proud of, but it was certainly true.

"I know," Simon agreed. "But in the long run, I think you're also better at taking care of yourself. The trouble with Nicole is that she always wants to be liked. She tries hard to please everyone, and she ends up going off in a dozen different directions at once. You know, she has to be the best student, the best athlete, the most popular."

Simon smiled. "Now you, on the other hand,

are the last person I know who would do something just because everyone else you knew was doing it. You always find your own way."

If you only knew! Sarah thought. Being an apprentice witch certainly was different, but there were times when Sarah wished she *could* be more like the rest of her friends.

Simon polished off the first half of his sandwich and sat back in his chair, smiling with satisfaction. It wasn't often that Sarah asked for his opinions, and he really enjoyed playing the all-knowing big brother.

Sarah decided to throw him a curve. "I've got another question for you," she said. "Do you think Aunt Pam used to be jealous of Mom?"

Simon had been leaning backward, balancing his chair on its back legs. The question caught him so much by surprise that he had to windmill his arms to keep from tipping over backward. "Where did you get that idea?" he asked.

"Oh, I don't know. Just something Aunt Pam said the other day."

Simon sat upright and pulled his chair close to the table. "The funny thing is, Mom did tell me a strange story about her and Aunt Pam when they were in high school. You know Mom has a beautiful soprano voice, but she never cared very much about performing in public.

Anyway, the year she was a junior, her school's drama club put on one of the those old-fashioned musical comedies. *The King and I*, I think it was. And Mom got the lead role!"

"So?" Sarah put in. "That's nice. But what's so strange about it?"

"Because," Simon said mysteriously, "she never tried out."

"I don't get it."

Simon smiled. "Don't you see. *Someone else* must have auditioned in her place."

Simon leaned over the table, sticking his face close to his sister's and hummed the *Twilight Zone* theme song. "Duh-da-duh-da-duh-da-duh-da."

"Stop that," Sarah begged. "Tell me the whole story."

Simon grinned. He liked nothing better than playing the expert. "Mom told me she always suspected Aunt Pam of going to the tryouts in her place. But she could never figure out how Aunt Pam could have gotten away with it. They looked sort of alike, but not enough to fool their teachers and classmates. Besides, Aunt Pam is an alto. She could never have sung Mom's music."

"So it would have been impossible," Sarah said. "Mom must be wrong." Of course, in her heart she knew better. "What did Mom do?"

she asked Simon. "Did she take the part?"

"Oh, sure," Simon said. "She would never have had the nerve to audition herself. But since she was already in the cast, she stuck with the play and had a great time."

"I wonder how Aunt Pam felt about that," Sarah mused out loud.

"That's a good question," said Simon. "But it's hard to imagine that Aunt Pamela had very many reasons to be jealous of Mom. I mean, she's had such an exciting life. You know, traveling, running a business, and so on."

More exciting than you think, Sarah added silently.

Sarah finished her sandwich and stacked the dirty plates in the dishwasher. Upstairs, she looked around for Bandit, the Connell's black cat. To her surprise, she found him stretched out on Nicole's bed. Nicole didn't like the cat to leave hairs on her bedspread, and Bandit had been chased out of her room so often that he normally avoided it entirely.

Tonight, the cat looked so comfortable lying there in the darkened room that Sarah didn't have the heart to pick him up. Instead she stretched out on the bed and stroked Bandit's chin. She suddenly felt very sleepy, and the cat's contented purring made her so logy she could hardly keep her eyes open.

Something warm and furry was nudging Sarah's shoulder. She opened her eyes and saw a pair of golden eyes staring intently down into her own.

"Bandit!" she cried, reaching out to scratch the cat's ears. "You scared me."

Pleased that she was awake, the cat climbed up onto her chest and settled down, purring loudly. Sarah took in her surroundings, wondering what she was doing in Nicole's bedroom.

She was still wearing the clothes she'd put on the evening before, so she must have dropped off when she was petting Bandit and slept straight through the night. The clock said seven A.M. which meant that she'd had a regular night's sleep, but she felt tired and grungy.

Pulling herself to her feet, she went into her own bedroom, grabbed her robe, and headed for the bathroom. Half an hour later, after a bracing shower, she felt much better, almost like her normal self. Dressing quickly in jeans and a man-tailored shirt, she carried her schoolbooks downstairs and spread them out on the kitchen table. By the time Simon came down an hour later, she had finished her homework for the weekend and was nearly finished reviewing for the next week's French quiz.

Simon blundered into the room, still barefoot

and rubbing the sleep from his bleary eyes. But the second he saw Sarah he did a double take.

"What got into you?" he demanded. "I can't believe you're doing homework at eight o'clock on a Saturday morning. What happened to your usual system of putting off your schoolwork until Sunday night?"

Sarah stared at the neat pile of books and papers in front of her. Why *was* she doing homework at this hour? "I don't know," she said lamely. "I just got this urge. It sort of came over me."

Simon laughed. "That sounds like the plot for a horror movie. I can see it now. A strange virus attacks otherwise normal teenagers, causing an uncontrollable urge to study. Now that's really creepy. A lot worse than being attacked by some bloodthirsty, ax-wielding madman, if you ask me."

"It sure would be," said Sarah. Simon's guess was a lot closer than he knew, and as far as she was concerned it was no laughing matter.

Simon was standing in front of the open refrigerator, digging out the eggs, a pound of bacon, and English muffins. Apparently, his late-night snack had done nothing to curb his appetite for a big breakfast. "You know," he said, "for a minute there, I actually thought you were Nicole. Not that you look like her, but in that shirt you're wearing and in those loafers, you reminded me of her."

Sarah glanced down at her feet. The loafers she had on were hers, but she hadn't worn them in ages. She must have dug them out of the back of her closet unconsciously.

This is getting too strange, she thought. It was bad enough when I couldn't control my appearance while I was being Nicole. But now I'm out of control when I'm just trying to be myself.

Refusing Simon's offer to cook her a plate of eggs and bacon, she got up from the table. "I think I'm going to bike over to Aunt Pam's and have morning tea with her."

Sarah's aunt Pam was only a few minutes away by bike, and Sarah arrived just in time to catch her aunt as she returned from her morning jog.

Even when she was exercising, Sarah's aunt managed to look glamorous. She was wearing a jogging suit made of purple velour material with gold trim, and spotless white running shoes. Tiny gold hoop-earrings set off her heart-shaped face and her glossy mane of black hair was pulled back into a pony tail.

Aunt Pam didn't seem surprised to see her niece. Without a word, she unlocked the shop door and led Sarah through the store and up the circular wrought-iron staircase to her apartment. Sarah waited while her aunt took a quick shower and brewed a pot of tea. As usual, just being in her aunt's place had a calming effect on her. The apartment was filled with giant throw pillows and invitingly comfortable furniture.

"Tell me, how is your experiment going?" Aunt Pam asked after Sarah had taken a few bracing sips of tea.

"Not so well." Sarah recounted the story of her evening at the movies. "It's bad enough that David and Micki are both angry with me," she concluded. "But now I'm starting to think like Nicole even when I'm myself. And that's scary. I've had enough of this spell. I want to end it."

Aunt Pam frowned. Sarah noticed that the ring her aunt wore, the one that seemed to change colors, had shifted from a clear blue to a shade of murky mauve.

"I warned you that it wouldn't be that easy," she reminded Sarah.

"You said that I would have to learn to see the world through Nicole's eyes," Sarah protested. "But I've done that, haven't I? You should have seen me mooning over Derek last night. Even Micki was disgusted."

"I'm sorry," her aunt commiserated, "but there's nothing I can do to get you out of this. There must be something you're supposed to do for Nicole. Something even I don't know. But I do know the spell won't be broken until you figure out what it is and do it."

Sarah had an idea. "Like the time you got Mom that role in the school musical."

Her aunt's almond-shaped eyes regarded her with curiosity. "How did you find out about that?"

"Simon told me," Sarah said. "He heard it from Mom. She's still trying to figure it out."

Aunt Pam laughed. "I was sure I'd be found out that time. Your mother really wanted that role, but she was too insecure to try out for it. I admit, though, that my motives weren't all that generous at first. I so much wanted to have a voice like Kate's that I wished I could be her. Then I went to the audition on impulse."

"But you didn't enjoy being Mom as much as you thought you would," Sarah guessed.

"That's right," her aunt agreed. "I had your mother's beautiful voice. But I also acquired her stage fright. I found out how much courage it takes to conquer an attack of nerves and sing in front of an audience. Your mother could overcome her nerves and go on once she knew everyone was counting on her. But I don't think

I would have been able to do it."

"That's something I never knew about Mom," Sarah said appreciatively. "But I don't see how what you learned applies to me. There's nothing I can do for Nicole."

"There must be something," her aunt said evenly. "And for once, I can't tell you the answer. You'll just have to see this through until you learn what it is."

Cycling home, Sarah wrestled with her feelings of disappointment. She'd been so sure that her aunt Pam would have the solution to her problem. Now she had no choice but to transform herself into Nicole again.

One consolation was that the next big event on Nicole's schedule was cheerleading practice. Sarah had always dreamed of being a varsity cheerleader herself someday. In fact, she and Micki had secretly borrowed Nicole's handbook and learned some of the routines just for fun. Actually getting to perform with the squad, even if it was just at practice, was going to be really exciting.

Maybe this spell isn't so bad after all, Sarah told herself as she shifted her bike into high gear. How many girls get to be a cheerleader even for a day? And this evening, I'll go to the dance with Derek.

Chapter 8

"The next part of the routine has ten jumping jacks," Miss Ramsey called out. "Nicole, remember to lift your right leg high. Then your left. This is called an attitude of the leg, so make it graceful."

"Right, Miss Ramsey," Sarah answered. She'd heard of good attitudes and bad attitudes, but never an attitude of the leg.

Cheerleading practice was barely under way, and already Sarah was beginning to wonder if she'd be able to bluff her way through the session. Instead of delivering the note excusing Nicole from practice, Sarah had just taken her sister's place. She had used another precious drop of her *Transformation* potion to make sure that she would be able to control her appearance. But cheerleading was turning out to be a lot tougher than she had expected.

Sarah considered herself in good shape. But the exercise routine that Miss Ramsey called a "warm up" was really demanding. After half an hour of aerobics, Sarah was ready for a break, but Miss Ramsey was still going strong. Not only that, the cheerleading coach was using a lot of specialized terms that Sarah had never heard before. Miss Ramsey taught ballet and modern dance as well as being the faculty adviser for the cheerleaders, and her manner made it clear that she took cheering every bit as seriously as a production of *Swan Lake*.

Sarah had positioned herself in the back row, where she could follow the moves made by the rest of the group. Still, every time Miss Ramsey announced a new combination of steps, Sarah crossed her fingers, hoping she wouldn't make too much of a fool out of herself.

So far, at least, none of the other cheerleaders showed any signs of suspecting that she wasn't really Nicole. Luckily, Sarah knew almost all of their names. But the member of the squad she'd heard the most about didn't show up until they had nearly finished their aerobic warm-up.

Candy Sweet — real name, Caroline Sweet — was a tall, leggy senior with tawny hair and hazel eyes. Unlike the other girls, who had shown up for practice in well-worn warm-up suits or running shorts, Candy was wearing a gold-and-blue striped spandex leotard and gold tights, a combination that did everything possible to show off her perfect figure.

Nicole Connell didn't like Candy very much, but Sarah had always assumed that her sister was just too preppy to appreciate Candy's flamboyant style. Now she wasn't so sure.

"Sorry about being late," Candy said, flashing an insincere smile in Miss Ramsey's direction as she took a place in the front row.

"No problem, dear," Miss Ramsey cooed back.

It was obvious that Candy was the coach's pet. But judging from the unsmiling faces of the rest of the squad, she wasn't about to win the Miss Congeniality award, if one were ever given out. Jenny Struthers, who was standing on the other side of Eric Rissom, actually made a face and pretended to stick a finger down her throat.

Maybe Jenny was just jealous. After all, Candy did sort of stand out from the group, and she was one of the leaders of the senior class besides. But Sarah was starting to think that there might be a good reason why the other members of the squad reacted the way they did. Candy certainly didn't act as if she really were sorry about coming in late.

"Now that we're all ready to begin," Miss Ramsey announced, "we can start to run through some actual cheers. We'll take turns acting as leader."

Miss Ramsey passed the megaphone to Stephanie Clark, in the front row, who immediately called for a locomotive. Sarah waited nervously for her turn to come around, hoping all the cheers she could think of wouldn't already be used up. When Craig Walters finally did pass the megaphone her way, the only cheer that came to mind was an old chestnut:

"Our team is red hot," she shouted.

"Their team is all shot," the squad continued.

"We haven't done that cheer in weeks," Stephanie laughed.

"Right," said Eric Rissom, "leave it to Nicole to remind us of the classics."

Sarah was starting to feel more relaxed. She remembered even more of the moves than she expected. In fact, it was almost as if she had acquired Nicole's reflexes along with her looks. Effortlessly, she leaped high in the air, performing straddle jumps, herkies, and other moves whose names she could barely recall.

And later, when the squad started working on a new routine for the next week's halftime show, she paired off with Eric, a tall, broad-shouldered boy whose huge hands easily encircled her waist. Sarah felt as if she were being partnered with King Kong at first. But Eric's strength and confidence took the fear out of tricky moves like the butterfly lift where he held her overhead while she arched her back in a graceful pose.

Sarah was really enjoying herself when Miss Ramsey announced that they would run through just one more routine before breaking for the day. "This is the entrance we're going to do at the beginning of the game, before we go into the Warriors' fight song," she explained. "You just do a series of cartwheels to get to your place in line."

That'll be a snap, Sarah told herself. At least, it would be as long as she had Nicole's reflexes going for her.

Candy happened to be in front of her as the squad lined up for the routine. Sarah watched as the flashy senior did a series of perfect cartwheels, finishing in exactly the right position. Then came her own turn. She started well, doing one . . . two . . . three complete revolutions. But as she came out of her last cartwheel, her feet failed to make contact with the ground. Instead of finishing her entrance with a sprightly smile, she found herself sprawled on her rear, her face contorted in a mask of surprise and outrage.

Candy Sweet had tripped her. Sarah was sure of it. As she struggled to her feet, she shot Candy a questioning look, but Candy pretended not to notice.

"Hey, don't just look the other way," Sarah challenged the senior girl. "You can at least tell me why you did that."

Candy answered with an insolent stare. "Don't blame me. I can't help it if you're clumsy," she retorted.

Unfortunately Miss Ramsey hadn't seen what happened. "It's bad enough that you fell," she told Sarah. "Don't compound your mistake by talking in the middle of a routine. When you're performing in public, you've got to try to recover from your mistakes and go on."

My mistakes! Sarah thought. That's a good one. But she forced herself to stifle her complaint and go on. Miss Ramsey seemed to mean well, but it was obvious that she had no idea what Candy was really like. She was one of those teachers who liked to think of herself as being really tuned in. But actually, she had no idea of what was going on right under her nose.

At long last, the coach called a five-minute

break, and Sarah joined Eric and Stephanie at the water cooler. "What's wrong with Candy?" she asked. "Am I crazy, or did she trip me on purpose?"

"I'm sure it was on purpose," Eric said. "Candy is being even nastier than usual today. You were looking awfully good on that last routine, and Candy doesn't like to be upstaged. Especially not today, with the election for squad captain coming up tomorrow."

Election? This was the first Sarah had heard of any election, but she was careful not to let on.

"I hate to think that Candy is going to win," Stephanie said, "but I don't see how it can be stopped. She's the chairman of the Spring Carnival committee and editor of the video yearbook. None of the seniors want to make her angry by running against her. It's easier just to let Candy have her way. She's been counting on being captain, and she can get really nasty when she's crossed."

"I can see how Candy could get back at the seniors," Sarah said, thinking out loud. "But what could she do to a junior?"

Stephanie and Eric stared at her. "Nothing, I guess," Eric mused. "But no junior has ever been squad captain. The seniors would never vote for one of us, even over Candy."

Maybe not, thought Sarah. Still, it was funny that neither Eric nor Stephanie had thought of running. It was almost as if the whole squad were used to being bullied by Candy.

Luckily, Sarah told herself silently, it isn't my problem.

When practice resumed after the break, Sarah made a point of standing at the far end of the line from Candy. She didn't want to cause any trouble that Nicole would have to take the blame for later. But Candy wasn't in an apologetic mood. "Watch your big feet this time," she warned Sarah as they lined up to practice the rest of the fight song routine.

"I'll watch my feet if you watch what you say," Sarah shot back automatically. It was too bad, she thought, that someone couldn't teach Candy a lesson.

Suddenly, Sarah had a wonderful idea. She kept her place in line and waved her pompons energetically, as she sang the familiar words of the Waterville fight song: "Fight, Warriors, fight. Struggle with all your might. . . ."

On the last line everyone jumped high in the air. Everyone, that is, except Candy, who did an awkward half-bounce, then started hopping jerkily from one foot to the other. "Hey, what's going on?" she yelped, staring down at her own feet.

Everyone else was looking at Candy's feet, too.

Eric was the first to laugh out loud. "How did you *do* that?" he snorted, pointing at the laces of Candy's shoes. The ends were neatly tied — to each other!

"I didn't do it," Candy whined. "Someone is playing a trick on me."

For once, Miss Ramsey wasn't taking her favorite's side. "Don't be silly," she snapped. "I was watching the group the whole time. Besides, no one could have tied your shoelaces together without your knowing it."

"But someone did," Candy insisted.

"No, they didn't," Miss Ramsey countered. "The laces just must have gotten tangled."

Candy saw that it was pointless to argue, but she sulked through the rest of the practice. She was sure that someone had tricked her. She even cast a few suspicious glances in Sarah's direction. But even she couldn't figure out how Sarah — or rather sweet, straight-arrow Nicole — could have managed such a thing.

When practice ended, Candy changed as quickly as possible and left the locker room without a word. As soon as the swinging doors closed behind her, the girls started buzzing. "That's the first time I ever saw Candy make a klutz of herself," one of the girls said with satisfaction. "Maybe now she'll have a little more sympathy for those of us who make mistakes once in a while."

"Don't count on it," said Tanya Rinaldi. "Remember, the election for captain is tomorrow. Candy will win, and then she'll lord it over us for the rest of the year."

"How come the election is tomorrow?" Sarah asked. "Isn't it strange to be voting for squad captain on Sunday?"

The girls all stared at her. "Because tomorrow's our annual squad brunch," she said. "At Miss Ramsey's house."

Sarah knew she had asked a stupid question. Naturally, Nicole must have known all about the brunch. "Oh, right," she said automatically.

"Aren't you coming?" Tanya asked.

Am I? Sarah wondered. Obviously, the real Nicole couldn't attend. She would still be in San Francisco with her mom and dad. But why hadn't she said anything about the brunch before she left? If attending had been really important to her, Dad probably wouldn't have forced her to go to San Francisco, Sarah thought. But she hadn't said a word.

All the girls were waiting to hear Sarah's answer, but she couldn't come up with any excuse for skipping the brunch that would have made sense. The easiest thing would be to say yes, she realized. She could always call Miss Ramsey the next day and claim to be ill.

"Sure, I'm coming," she said. "But I still don't understand why everyone's ready to cave in and let Candy be squad captain."

Tanya was in front of the big mirror, studiously applying a curling iron to add frizz to her straight blonde hair. "Personally, I want to be on the Spring Carnival committee. Anyway, squad captain is mostly an honorary post. If it makes Candy happy to think she's queen of the cheerleaders, then let her."

That sounded like sour grapes to Sarah. She would have liked to argue, but she was afraid to hang around the locker room any longer than necessary. Practice had taken more time than she expected. Studying herself in the mirror, Sarah could see that her image was already starting to get a bit hazy around the edges. Furthermore, her hair was just a shade darker than it had been when practice began.

It was amazing that none of the other girls had noticed. But then, as Sarah was beginning to see, changing from one person to another was a lot easier to get away with than anyone realized. Even if Nicole's friends noticed something not quite right about her looks, they wouldn't be likely to guess that the person they were calling Nicole was really Sarah. More likely, they'd just think Nicole hadn't had much sleep the night before. Or had fixed her hair differently. It didn't occur to people to suspect that their friends were not really who they seemed to be.

Still, Sarah reminded herself, there was no sense in pushing her luck. There were only a few drops left of the potion Aunt Pam had given her, and she didn't want to waste any of them now that practice was officially over.

Stuffing her practice clothes hastily into her gym bag, Sarah said good-bye to the other girls and hurried out of the locker room. She was waiting at the bus stop, sure that she'd made a timely exit, when a sporty red Honda pulled up with Stephanie Clarke behind the wheel.

"Come on," she shouted, "hop in. I'll drive you home."

Sarah couldn't think of an excuse to say no. And she probably wouldn't have used it if she had. Riding in Stephanie's new car was a lot more fun than taking the bus. Nicole and her friends didn't appreciate how lucky they were to be juniors. It was really gross being thirteen and having to use public transportation or rely on your parents to ferry you around.

Stephanie slipped a Bon Jovi tape into the tape deck and turned up the volume. As they drove through the village, they passed a few groups of kids from school, headed for the ice-cream store on the corner or doing Saturday errands. Sarah was having a great time. Her only regret was that she couldn't show off to her friends. Even if they saw her riding with Stephanie they wouldn't know who she really was.

Just as she was resigning herself to the situation, Micki came out of the drugstore, carrying two heavy-looking plastic bags.

"Hey, there's Micki Davis," Sarah exclaimed. "Let's offer her a ride."

Stephanie was not overjoyed. "You mean that red-headed girl who hangs around with your kid sister? Why?"

"Come on, Steph. She's got a lot of stuff to carry," Sarah urged.

"Okay. If you want to."

They stopped at the corner, and Sarah excitedly motioned to Micki to get in. She squeezed in next to Sarah in the front seat, looking almost as doubtful as Stephanie.

"Let's drive the long way around to my house," Sarah suggested. "We can go past the mini-mall."

"Whatever." Stephanie shrugged.

While Stephanie concentrated on her driving and singing along with her tape, Micki was nudging Sarah. "What's going on?" she mouthed silently.

Sarah felt mildly annoyed. She had wanted to treat Micki to a ride in Stephanie's car as a way of making up for their quarrel. But Micki didn't seem capable of just relaxing and enjoying herself.

A few minutes later, they reached the neighborhood where Sarah and Micki both lived. "You can just let me out at the Connell house," Micki told Stephanie. "There's something I want to see Sarah about."

Stephanie looked surprised. "Is she home? I thought Nicole said something about her sister being away for the weekend."

"Oh, she'll be home soon," Micki said. "I'm sure of it."

They stopped in front of the Connell driveway. Micki looked as if she could hardly wait for Stephanie to leave, and Sarah was so annoyed that she made a point of taking her time saying good-bye.

When Stephanie finally drove away, she turned to face her friend. "What's wrong with you?" she demanded. "Why did you say that about me being home? I thought you were going to give away my secret right there in the car."

"*Me* give it away!" Micki said indignantly.

Before she could say any more, they were interrupted by the appearance of Simon, coming down the street on his ten-speed bike.

Sarah gasped. Simon, of all people, knew that Nicole was out of town. But there was nowhere to hide. No time to change her appearance.

As he turned into the driveway, Sarah stood waiting for him, wondering how she was ever going to explain.

"I guess you caught me this time," she said.

Simon looked bewildered. "Caught you doing what, Sarah?"

Chapter 9

Simon disappeared into the house, and Sarah gave herself a quick once over. Her feet were her own. So were her hands. Her hair had returned to its natural dark shade. Only her clothes — the jeans with the carefully ironed creases and the oxford cloth shirt-blouse — were still one-hundred percent Nicole.

"What happened?" Sarah asked.

"I was trying to *tell* you," Micki giggled. "The spell wore off. You were changing right there in the car. I can't believe Stephanie didn't notice."

"But she didn't, did she?" Sarah pointed out. "That just proves my theory. People see what they expect to see. They don't believe in magic, so it can happen right in front of their eyes and they don't even notice it."

Micki groaned. "Maybe that works with Stephanie Clarke. I don't think she's exactly the most observant person in the world. Boys, cars, and music are all she cares about. Not necessarily in that order. But I wouldn't count on getting away with that in front of anyone else."

"Come on, Micki," Sarah cajoled. "Be loose. You're taking all this too seriously. Let's go up to my room and chill out."

Sarah grabbed some apples and oranges from the fruit bowl in the kitchen and led the way to her room. Micki settled on the peach bedspread next to Bandit, who immediately curled up in her lap, purring softly.

"Call me a killjoy," Micki said. "But I wish you would give up this game. There have been too many close calls. You'll never make it to tomorrow night."

"I can't give it up."

Sarah explained what she'd learned from her aunt Pam about the spell. "There's something I have to do. Something Nicole wants to do, but can't manage to do for herself."

"But what is it?" Micki asked. "And how will you know you're working things out the way Nicole would want them?"

Sarah shrugged. "So far, I don't know. But I have a few hints. First, there's this election for cheerleading captain at Miss Ramsey's brunch tomorrow. It's funny that Nicole seems to have forgotten all about it. But now that I attended practice, I'll have to show up at Miss Ramsey's.

"Next," she went on, "there's my date with Derek tonight. He kept hinting that there's something important he wants to discuss. But I still don't know what it is."

"Maybe he wants Nicole to go steady with him," Micki suggested. Then she rolled her eyes as another thought crossed her mind. "Or maybe it's something even more serious than that."

Sarah bit into an apple thoughtfully. "It'd better not be. I can't even make up my mind what I *think* about Derek. When I'm around him, he seems really special. But sometimes I wonder if that's just the spell working a little too well."

"I'm glad I'm not an apprentice witch," Micki sighed. "It's exciting and all that, but if you make a mistake and mess up Nicole's life, she might never forgive you."

Sarah had been thinking the same thing. "I wish you were going to be at this community center dance tonight. Why don't you come?"

"I don't have a date, for one thing." Micki pointed out. "And no one I know is going. I'm not about to show up alone."

"You could call Rick and ask him," Sarah suggested.

"I can't do that!" Micki looked horrified. "We just went out for the first time last night. And it wasn't exacly the most successful date of all time, if you'll recall."

"I guess not."

"Besides," Micki added. "It's a costume party, and I wouldn't know what to wear."

"It is?" That was the first time Sarah had heard about having to dress up. She'd been planning to wear casual clothes.

"Sure," Micki informed her. "It's the community center's twentieth anniversary. So they're having a sixties party. Everyone's supposed to pretend it's 1968."

Sarah finished her apple and pitched the core into the wastebasket. "At least that solves the problem of having to wear Nicole's clothes. They're almost like a costume, in a way. I always feel as if I've just stepped out of a J. Crew catalogue."

"Maybe we could go up to the attic and see what your mom has in her old trunks," Micki suggested. "I bet there's lots of stuff there that would be good for the party."

Fortunately, Sarah's mom was a pack rat. Since Sarah's father had his offices at home, the Connells lived in a big old house, and the substantial attic was stuffed to the rafters with out-of-date possessions that Mrs. Connell had never been able to bring herself to pack off to the Salvation Army. Within minutes Sarah and Micki had located a trunk filled with clothes that dated back to Kate Connell's college days.

"Look at this!" Micki cried, holding up a long dress made of thin Indian cotton. "Can you believe your mom actually wore this? It's the same kind of material my bedspread at camp was made of."

Micki tried the dress on, and whirled around in front of the old stand-up mirror in the corner. "Weird as it is, it fits me," she observed.

"You might as well keep it," Sarah said. "Maybe you can use it for Halloween sometime. That is, if you don't change your mind and come to the dance tonight after all."

Sarah, meanwhile, had unearthed a pile of other strange items — platform sandals with two-inch thick soles, tie-dyed T-shirts in orange-and-yellow sunburst designs, dangling earrings made of colored glass beads, even an enormous stained-glass peace symbol attached to a leather thong.

"You're right," she told Micki. "I'm not sure I'd have the nerve to appear in public in some of this stuff. Even for a costume party."

After a little searching, however, she dug

out a long, flared skirt and a gauzey Indian cotton blouse that didn't look too bad on her. The platform sandals were a little small, but once she had changed to become Nicole, they would probably fit perfectly.

"Here, try these," Micki suggested. She handed Sarah a pair of rimless granny glasses with blue-tinted lenses.

"Now I really do look weird," Sarah said. "I wonder what Derek is going to wear to this party."

"And I wonder what he'll say when he sees Nicole dressed like this," Micki added.

At first, Derek didn't say anything at all. When he showed up at the Connell house that evening driving his dad's car, Sarah was watching for him from her bedroom window. Even before his car came to a stop, she had dabbed a drop of her *Transformation* potion behind her ear and pulled on her party clothes. She managed to get outside and safely into the car before Simon, who was in his own room listening to some tapes, had a chance to see her.

"Hey-up," Derek said by way of greeting as she slid into the front seat next to him.

He wasn't in costume, but it didn't really matter. Derek's school T-shirt and jeans would have fit in any era. And with his dreamy good looks, it wouldn't make any difference what he wore.

The trouble was, Sarah was so hypnotized by Derek's looks that she couldn't think of a thing to say. She wondered what he and Nicole usually talked about on dates. School work? Sports?

"What did you do today?" she said finally.

It wasn't a very original question, but at least it broke the ice.

"Worked out at the gym," Derek said. "I'm up to fifty pounds on my arm curls with the Nautilus machines. Thirty repetitions. And two hundred pounds bench pressing with free weights. Then I ran three miles on the indoor track. . . ."

Derek went on for about ten minutes, describing his workout in excruciating detail. Sarah tried her best to look interested.

They had reached the parking lot of the community center before Derek finished his account and seemed to notice his date for the first time. "Hey, Nicole," he said. "How come you're dressed like that?"

"This is my sixties costume," Sarah explained. "I thought I did a pretty good job of putting it together. My mom used to wear these clothes when she was in college."

Derek blinked. "A costume? Oh, right."

Sarah was relieved when they got inside to see that the dance actually was a costume party. The center was decorated with old psychedelic posters and the sound system was playing a Mamas and Papa's song, "California Dreamin' ".

Stephanie Clarke was wearing a beaded vest over a peasant blouse and a long skirt. Candy Sweet had come in a miniskirt and white boots, with a pink crocheted top. Nicole's best friend, Kerry, was wearing a tie-dyed shirt with bell-bottom jeans. Lots of the girls had come in variations on this costume. Most of the boys weren't dressed up at all.

Derek went off to get some sodas, and Sarah sat down at a table with Kerry and Jonathan Durham.

"I like your outfit," Kerry volunteered.

Sarah smiled. She had had a lot of fun putting her costume together and she was pleased with the way she looked. Nicole's straight blonde hair, parted in the middle, looked very sixties, she thought.

"This is kind of fun," Sarah said. "I keep trying to imagine what my parents must have looked like dressed like this."

Kerry giggled. "I hadn't thought of that. But do you know what? My dad used to have a beard! I saw this picture of him in my grand-mother's scrapbook."

"And my dad had sideburns," Sarah con-fessed. "They were big and bushy and came all the way down to his jaw. It was gross!"

Derek had returned to the table, but he made no effort to join the conversation. "Who cares what our folks used to look like?" he said. "That's all ancient history. Right?"

He turned to Jonathan and starting describ-ing his afternoon workout, going through the same list of exercises he had just described in the car.

Just when Sarah was about to scream with boredom, she saw Micki coming in the front door of the hall. She was wearing the Indian print dress she had found in the Connell attic and Rick was with her.

Sarah excused herself from the table and went over to say hello to her friend. Even though they had both laughed at the old dress at first, it made Micki look strangely pretty, almost exotic. The bright colors made her com-plexion look even more perfect than usual, and Micki had crimped her red hair until it stood out around her head in a burnished halo.

"I don't know how you managed to trick Rick into inviting me," she whispered to Sarah. "I almost said no. But I decided to come out of curiosity."

"I didn't have anything to do with it!" Sarah protested. "Honest, Micki. Rick must have just asked you on his own. I mean, I would have tried to get him to invite you, but I wasn't sure you even liked him."

Micki's expression showed that she didn't believe her friend for a minute. "That's all right," she said, squeezing Sarah's elbow. "I'm not sure I'm all that crazy about Rick, either. But it's more fun being here than spending Saturday night at home alone watching TV."

Sarah gave up. One of the problems with being an apprentice witch was that Micki seemed to think she was responsible for everything that happened. And this time at least, it wasn't true. The problem wasn't so much that Micki didn't like Rick as that Sarah didn't like him. So after Micki had turned down her suggestion about asking Rick to the dance, Sarah had forgotten all about it.

To tell the truth, she'd sort of forgotten about Micki altogether. She'd been so wrapped up in thinking about her experiment of pretending to be Nicole that she had forgotten that she had been supposed to go over to Micki's house to watch Crypt Classics, the Saturday night horror film festival that was featured on one of the local TV stations.

"So tell me," Micki asked eagerly, "what's it like being out with Derek?"

"So far, it's boring," Sarah admitted. "We don't seem to have much to talk about. All he's interested in is his muscles."

"That's all half the girls at Waterview High are interested in, too," Micki pointed out. "Anyway, no one ever said Derek was a great talker. You're supposed to be dancing with him."

"I guess so," Sarah said. "I'd better get back to where we're sitting."

Micki suddenly looked stern. "Have a good time. But remember, he's Nicole's boyfriend. And David is yours. Or at least I think he still is."

Leave it to Micki, Sarah thought, to inject a thudding note of reality into every situation. She'd managed to put her quarrel with David completely out of her mind. And she wasn't about to start worrying about that now. David was working tonight at the Pizza Palace.

And anyway, he'd never know what she was doing tonight. As far as the world knew, she was Nicole Connell, high school junior, out on a date with her usual boyfriend.

Come to think of it, Sarah mused, I'm really lucky. Lots of girls have wished they could split themselves in half so they could have a steady boyfriend and still have a chance to date other guys, just to see what they're like. This is my chance. So why am I worrying so much instead of having a good time?

Returning to Derek and the others, she managed to tear him away from his discussion of Nautilus routines by suggesting that they dance. A slow number was playing, an old Dionne Warwick song. Derek planted his large hand around Sarah's waist and steered her out onto the dance floor.

Derek was not a great dancer by any means. But once she was close to him, Sarah felt the familiar, weak-in-the-knees feeling returning.

What's more, as the two of them moved slowly across the dance floor, Sarah had the unfamiliar sensation of being the center of attention. It didn't take ESP to know that everyone in the room was thinking that she and Derek made the perfect couple. Sure, there were lots of good-looking kids at the dance. But Nicole's blonde, blue-eyed prettiness and Derek's Greek-god profile belonged in another league. And when the two of them were together, the effect was even more dazzling.

Sarah knew that in theory looks weren't important. She could just imagine what her mom would say if she tried to explain what she was feeling now. "You have a warped sense of values, Sarah," was one phrase that came to mind. Her aunt Pam would probably tell her the same thing. And for that matter, a few days ago she would have been the first to agree that Nicole put too much emphasis on appearances.

Now that she was in her sister's place, she wasn't sure she agreed. Who wouldn't want to be one half of the perfect couple, given the chance? Sarah felt a surge of giddy confidence, unlike anything she had ever felt before.

Chapter 10

All too soon the strains of the slow ballad faded away. That was when Sarah learned that her Greek god didn't go in for fast dancing.

"But Derek," she pleaded, "I'm really in the mood to dance tonight! Can't you at least try?"

"Aw come on, you know I'm a lousy dancer," he argued.

"Don't be silly. Anyone can dance, at least a little bit. No one expects you to be Michael Jackson."

Derek grudgingly returned to the dance floor. But in a few minutes it was obvious that he hadn't been exaggerating about being a lousy dancer. Derek's weightlifting had made him strong, but it hadn't done anything to make him graceful. He moved like a prize fighter dodging his opponent, Sarah thought, suppressing a giggle. Or worse, like a dancing bear.

They stuck it out for one song before Sarah suggested that they give up.

"Let's get some food," Derek said, motioning in the direction of the buffet table.

Derek was always hungry, but Sarah didn't feel like eating. "You go ahead," she said. "I'll go to the ladies' room and join you later."

As usual, the lounge area of the restroom was filled with girls who were fussing with their hair while they gossiped and discussed their dates. Sarah was surprised though, to find Kerry sitting alone on a cracked plastic couch in the corner. Kerry was one of those people who seemed to have been born cheerful. But tonight, she was looking uncharacteristically glum.

"What's wrong?" Sarah said, sitting down next to her.

Kerry made a face. "Candy, that's what's wrong."

At first, Sarah didn't understand. "Are you sick?" she asked. "What did you eat?"

Kerry grimaced. "Very funny. I'm sick to my stomach all right. But it isn't something I ate. It's Candy Sweet who's getting to me. I'm with Jonathan tonight, and you should see how she's moving in on him. You wouldn't believe the nerve of that girl."

"Oh, yes I would," Sarah assured her. She'd already seen Candy at work earlier in the day. "I wouldn't put anything past her. She's a shark."

Kerry sighed. "You said it. I'm sure she's not even interested in Jonathan. Not seriously. She just enjoys proving that she can get any guy she wants. It's the hunt she likes. If they're not with some other girl, she isn't interested."

"Well, one thing's sure," Sarah said. "You can't compete with Candy hiding out here in the ladies' room. Let's get going."

Kerry stared at her friend. Sarah guessed that this was not the advice Nicole would have given. She had already learned that Nicole, who could be so bossy at home, was not quite the same around her friends.

But even though Kerry looked doubtful, she ran a brush through her hair and followed her friend back to the table in the corner where Jonathan and Candy were sitting.

"Hi there," Candy greeted them, flashing a smile that made Sarah think of the great white shark in the *Jaws* movies. "Back from re-doing your makeup?" She studied them critically. "It *does* look a little better."

Candy liked to pretend that she didn't wear

makeup. From the way she talked, she was the original California sunshine girl. Sarah, who had seen Candy's gym bag in the locker room at cheerleading practice, knew better. Worse yet, Candy's year-round golden tan came out of a bottle. Sarah had nothing against makeup, but she thought that was going a little too far.

"Candy's been telling me about the Spring Carnival committee," Jonathan informed Kerry and Sarah. "It seems they need volunteers."

Candy's smile froze. "We need *guys* to volunteer," she corrected him, batting her long, curly eyelashes. "Our first job is to raise funds. And of course, males are so much *smarter* when it comes to finances." She fastened her long, claw-like fingernails around Jonathan's arm. "This budget stuff makes my head ache. But I'm sure you could explain it to me."

Incredibly, Jonathan seemed to be buying this line. Kerry looked ready to explode. She had been helping Jonathan with his algebra homework all year. But Jonathan seemed to have conveniently forgotten that. "I'm the one who gets A's in math," she informed Candy. "Any time you want the mystery of numbers explained to you, I'll be glad to help. No need to bother Jonathan."

"Oh, it's no bother," Jonathan said quickly.

He was so far gone that he didn't even seem to notice the sarcasm in Kerry's voice.

Sarah said nothing. She was still trying to imagine Candy Sweet as a shark. The comparison was amazingly accurate, now that she thought about it. Up close, Candy was not really as gorgeous as she seemed at first glance. Her eyes were a little too small. Her chin was weak, almost receding. And she had a slight overbite.

On the other hand, Candy was smooth like a shark. Smooth and sleek and streamlined. And slippery, too, Sarah thought.

While Candy prattled on about the Spring Carnival, Sarah found herself rearranging Candy's features. Then she tried picturing her with a zit. An ugly zit on her nose.

Sarah was so absorbed in her fantasy that she was the last to notice that is was coming true at that very moment. While Jonathan and Kerry watched, their eyes riveted on Candy's face, an actual pimple was forming on the tip of her nose. In a matter of seconds it grew from a tiny pink dot the size of a pinhead, to a menacing-looking pink-and-white blemish, the king of all zits.

Candy had no idea what was happening. But she couldn't help noticing that everyone at the table was suddenly watching her nose in absolute fascination. "What's going on?" she laughed. "What's the joke? You're playing some kind of trick on me, right?"

Jonathan looked embarrassed. "Of course not. I'm sorry."

Candy put a hand to her nose. By now, the zit was so big she could feel it. "Excuse me," she said, "I'm going to the ladies' room."

Candy fled from the table and Kerry flashed Sarah a grin of triumph. "I guess luck was on my side tonight," she whispered out of Jonathan's hearing. "I bet that's the first zit Candy ever had in her whole life. Imagine it breaking out like that right here at the dance!"

Sarah almost had to bite her tongue to keep from laughing. It was true that pimples always seemed to appear at the worst possible times. But even so, no real-life pimple could grow that bad in thirty seconds. Jonathan and Kerry both had seen something happen that was impossible. But their brains just refused to acknowledge the fact.

Candy, however, wasn't fooled. Sarah was on her way to the buffet table, looking for Derek, when Candy swooped down on her, looking furious. Candy had done her best to camouflage the pimple under several layers of makeup, but somehow the cosmetics only made the blemish more nasty-looking.

"You did this!" she said accusingly, pointing to her nose.

Sarah did her best to look innocent. "Are you out of your mind? How could I make your face break out?"

For once, Candy looked unsure of herself. "I can't explain it," she admitted. "But I just know you're responsible somehow. You're such a brain, you probably got hold of some chemical that produces instant zits and slipped it in my glass of punch."

Candy was talking so loud that everyone in the vicinity of the refreshment tables could hear her. A couple of seniors snickered. "Good thinking, Candy," one of them said.

Candy looked more annoyed than ever. She definitely was not a girl with a sense of humor, especially about herself. "Believe me, I won't forget this," she hissed.

Sarah watched wordlessly as Candy grabbed her belongings and sailed out the door of the community center — the great man-eating shark swimming out to sea.

Micki had seen the encounter from a distance. As soon as Candy was gone, she came up to Sarah and offered her a paper cup full of fruit punch. "Are you sure that was a good idea?" she asked. "Not that Candy didn't deserve it. But remember, tomorrow she's going to be elected cheerleading captain, and Nicole's the one who'll have to deal with it."

"Maybe you're right," Sarah said. "But I just couldn't resist. Anyway, there's nothing I can do about it now."

With Candy gone, the second half of the dance was even more fun than the first. Derek still didn't want to try fast dancing, but Sarah had no trouble finding partners. She danced once or twice with Jonathan, with Eric Rissom, and with several senior guys.

Strangest of all, she even danced with Kirk Tanner, from her own class. Judging from the puzzled look on his face, Kirk was madly trying to figure out why Nicole Connell, a popular junior, had suddenly taken an interest in him.

It was such a perfect opportunity that Sarah couldn't resist flirting a little. "You're a terrific dancer," she confided breathlessly, as they recovered from one very fast Rolling Stones number.

"Am I?" Kirk said, grinning from ear to ear. "I mean, I am. Thanks for noticing."

So much for Kirk's attempt to play the suave man of the world, Sarah thought mischievously. Kirk would probably follow Nicole around like a puppy dog for the next two weeks. And poor Nicole would have no idea what she had done to inspire his devotion.

When the final set started, Sarah didn't see Derek anywhere around. She finally found him in a far corner of the hall, near the DJ's station, deep in conversation with a couple of guys from the football team.

"Hey, Derek," she cajoled. "I know you don't exactly love dancing, but let's dance the last set together. Okay?"

Derek didn't look exactly thrilled, but once again he followed Sarah out onto the floor. Fortunately most of the songs in the set were slow tunes. Sarah rested her cheek against the sleeve of Derek's T-shirt.

"I really had a good time tonight," she said. "This had been a lot of fun."

Derek looked down at her, his blue eyes suddenly serious. "I guess that gives me a good idea of how you're going to answer my question," he said.

"Question?" Sarah asked. "What question?"

Suddenly her high spirits were punctured. This was the moment she had been dreading. Once again, she hadn't remembered to pump Kerry for advance information.

Worst of all, at that very moment, Sarah felt her feet and hands starting to tingle again — the signal that had warned her before that her shape-changing spell was beginning to wear off.

All she needed was to start changing back into her own body at the very moment when Derek was trying to have his serious discussion!

Desperately, she thought of the transformation potion that Aunt Pam had given her.

As subtly as possible, Sarah reached into the pocket of her skirt where she had hidden the glass perfume vial. With luck, she ought to be able to manage to dab on a teeny drop of the magic liquid without Derek noticing what she was doing. But her fingers failed to close around the precious vial.

Her pocket was empty.

Chapter 11

"Are you listening to me?" Derek demanded.

Sarah stared into the depths of Derek's blue eyes. Suddenly she knew how Cinderella must have felt at the royal ball when she looked at the clock and realized that it was five minutes to midnight. But Cinderella had it easy. All she had to worry about was her carriage turning into a pumpkin.

Her mind racing, Sarah tried to picture what would happen if she suddenly reverted to her own identity right there on the dance floor. Once before — the time she accidentally wished that Waterview High would disappear — her aunt Pam had helped her to straighten out the mess she had made. But her aunt had left no doubt that she wouldn't rescue Sarah every time she got into trouble.

"Part of being an apprentice witch," Aunt

Pam had told her after that incident, "is learning not to get involved in spells you can't control."

Of course, this time, it wasn't just her own life that was involved. Nicole would suffer, too. This was just the worst possible moment for a heart-to-heart talk with Derek. She could almost feel the roots of her hair turning dark. And her feet were growing bigger by the minute. Pretty soon her sandals would be so tight that she would scarcely be able to dance.

"Do we have to discuss this right this minute?" Sarah pleaded. "I think I lost something."

But Derek was in no mood to hear excuses, even reasonable ones. "You'll lose a boyfriend if you keep running away every time I try to talk to you seriously," Derek warned. "So let's stop fooling around."

That was the longest speech Sarah had ever heard him make on a subject other than exercise. She decided that she'd better stop worrying about her potion and pay attention.

"Okay," she said resignedly, "so what's your question?"

That obviously was not the right thing to say. Derek glowered. "We've discussed this a dozen times. How can you pretend you don't know what I want?"

Good grief, Sarah thought, Derek certainly

wasn't making this easy. Why was it that so many boys seemed to think that having to put their thoughts into words was a kind of defeat?

"Look, I'm not pretending," she said. "Honest. You've asked me lots of questions. I mean, just this evening you wanted to know whether I preferred diet soda or regular. I need to be sure we've both got the same question in mind."

Derek looked exasperated. "You know. I want to know your decision about quitting cheerleading."

"Quitting cheerleading?" Sarah repeated the question automatically, knowing she must sound and look like a total idiot.

"Come on, Nicole. Don't make this so tough on me," Derek complained. "You know why. It's nice having a girlfriend who's a cheerleader. I'm really proud of you. But I'm also tired of never having a date for the games. My buddies all go with their girlfriends, and I end up tagging along."

Sarah's first thought was that Derek's complaint made sense. Going to games alone would get to be a drag after a while. For that matter, she wasn't all that sure which she would prefer in Nicole's place. Being a cheerleader was fantastic, of course. But sitting in the bleachers with Derek wouldn't be bad, either.

Derek had made his point. But now that he had started talking, he couldn't seem to stop. "It just isn't fair," he went on. "I don't object to all the time you spend studying so you can be on the honor roll. I don't interfere with your being on the diving team. . . ."

Sarah had been ready to tell Derek what he wanted to hear. Now, she stopped short. "What do you mean 'interfere'?" she asked. "You couldn't interfere if you wanted to. It's my decision if I want to be on the diving team. You couldn't stop me."

"That's what I said," Derek insisted. "I didn't try to stop you."

"You're impossible, Derek Crawford. You're nothing but a. . . ." Sarah couldn't think of a name bad enough. Searching her mind, she settled on the insult her mother would have used. "You're a male chauvinist, that's what you are!"

Derek wasn't a quick thinker, and he still wasn't sure what he'd said to cause such an explosion. As his date fled the dance floor, he watched her go with a perplexed expression on his face. Not only was Nicole acting strangely tonight, she didn't look like herself either.

After breaking away from Derek, Sarah made a beeline for the corner of the hall where

Micki and Rick were dancing. Grabbing Micki's elbow, she hissed, "I've got to talk to you. It's an emergency."

"Now?" Micki and her date asked in unison. But Micki, who had been Sarah's best friend long enough to be used to her emergencies, allowed herself to be led off the dance floor.

"Something awful has happened," Sarah told her. "I lost the secret potion that Aunt Pam gave me. It was in the pocket of my skirt earlier in the evening. And now it's just gone!"

Micki's large brown eyes looked Sarah up and down. "That's too bad," she commiserated. "But you don't really need that stuff to change shapes, do you? When this got started, you were able to make the switch without any help at all."

Sarah didn't find the reminder at all comforting. "I know I did," she agreed, "but I'm not sure I could do it again. It seems as if this spell gets harder to control all the time. Especially when I'm Nicole."

"I guess we'd better look for that vial of potion," Micki agreed. "Your looks are fading fast."

Micki offered to search the dance floor and the area around the refreshment table, while Sarah checked out the restroom. She had a vague memory of having the vial in her pocket while she was talking to Kerry on the plastic couch in the ladies' room lounge. Maybe it had fallen down behind one of the cushions.

Sarah had hoped to find the ladies' room empty. But when she pushed open the door, she realized that she had interrupted an animated discussion between Kerry and Stephanie.

"Is that what you're looking for?" Kerry asked, holding out the vial.

"Yes, I lost it when I was in here before."

Sarah had reached out to grab the vial, but Kerry pulled it back, examining the label carefully for the first time.

"I don't think I ever heard of this scent before," she said. "What is this? One of those samples that they give out in the stores sometimes?" She held the vial up to the light. "Funny color. Mind if I try a drop?"

"No!" Sarah yelped. "I mean, yes! I do mind." She snatched the vial out of Kerry's hand.

Kerry looked so astonished that Sarah realized she had better come up with an excuse.

"I'm sorry," she said quickly. "But this isn't ordinary perfume. It's . . . it's a prescription."

"Prescription perfume?" Kerry wrinkled her nose.

Sarah thought fast. "Right. See, I dab it on

and it gets absorbed through my skin. And it makes me feel, uh, less dizzy."

Obviously, Kerry didn't believe a word of this. But she must have figured that it was pointless to argue. "You certainly need something to make you less dizzy," she said sarcastically. "What's wrong with you lately, Nicole? You look strange. Even your hair looks different. It's this dingy color. . . ."

Dingy! Sarah checked her appearance in the mirror. There was nothing dingy about her hair. It was just changing back from Nicole's insipid blonde shade to her own natural chestnut color. She wanted to give Kerry a piece of her mind, but she realized she had probably revealed too much already. "It's nothing serious," she said automatically. "I tried this new kind of rinse and it didn't work out so well, that's all."

"But you've been acting funny, too," Stephanie put in. "You're usually so calm and quiet. But lately you've been jumpy and strange."

"Right," Kerry put in. "For example, why are you spending so much time hanging around with your sister's friends? Derek said you were at the movies with them last night. And tonight I saw you dancing with Kirk Tanner."

"That's just the beginning," Stephanie continued. "Even though I can't figure out how you did it, I just know that you played that trick on Candy this morning. Tying her shoelaces together! Not that she didn't have it coming. But it isn't like you to pull a stunt like that."

Sarah could almost see the little wheels turning inside Kerry's head. So far, it hadn't occurred to Kerry that her friend might actually be responsible for making Candy's face break out tonight. Now, having heard Stephanie's accusation, she was beginning to put two and two together.

Sarah recalled a saying that Simon often used: The best *defense* is a good *offense*. For once, she had to admit that her brother was no dummy. If she kept on letting Stephanie and Kerry interrogate her, she was going to talk herself into trouble fast. She had to change the subject.

"You have a lot of nerve calling me strange when you two just sit back and let Candy push you around without doing a thing to stop her," she said accusingly. "Kerry, you weren't doing a thing to stop her from taking Jonathan away from you." She turned to Stephanie. "And I still don't understand why you are willing to let Candy get herself elected cheerleading squad captain."

Stephanie sighed. "For one thing, Candy is Miss Ramsey's favorite. If she gets in, we'll have smooth sailing for the rest of the year."

"That's a reason?" Sarah was outraged.

"Okay," Stephanie concluded. "I admit it. The real reason is that no one has the nerve to run against Candy. We all know that if she doesn't win, she'll make our lives miserable from now on."

"Maybe I'll run."

The words hung there in the stuffy air of the windowless lounge. Sarah had no recollection of ever saying them, but they had indeed come out of her mouth. Or rather, Nicole's mouth.

Stephanie looked shocked, then intrigued. "You know, that might not be such a bad idea. You're usually such a team player. I bet some of the seniors would even vote for you. If we could get Miss Ramsey to agree to a secret ballot, that is."'

On the spot, Stephanie outlined her ideas for getting Nicole elected. She was even willing to do some behind-the-scenes campaigning, provided of course that Candy didn't realize what was going on.

Stephanie left the room, already planning how she could maneuver Eric Rissom into putting Nicole's name into nomination.

"I still think you're out of your mind," Kerry said, unimpressed. "Derek might change his mind about wanting you to quit cheerleading.

But I know he won't like it one bit if you decide to run for captain. He'll think you're doing it just to spite him."

Sarah laughed weakly. "He won't think that," she said.

But in her heart, Sarah knew Kerry was right. So far, she had done a fantastic job of messing up her sister's life. Nicole hadn't fought her father's decision to take her away for the weekend because she wanted an excuse to avoid making a choice between Derek and cheerleading.

Now, with my help, Sarah thought glumly, Nicole may never have to make that choice at all. The way things are going, Derek will never speak to her again. And if Candy loses the election, she will probably find a way to drive Nicole off the squad.

Out in the main hall of the center, the dance was breaking up. The DJ had finished his last set and was packing his tapes into a silver metal case. Someone had turned up the lights, and the decorations, which had seemed funky and fun just a few minutes earlier, looked cheap and forlorn.

There is nothing sadder than party decorations after the party is over, Sarah thought.

She had used another precious dab of the

Transformation potion to restore her appearance as Nicole. But even so, she was feeling tired and bedraggled. Her feet ached from dancing all night in her mother's ridiculous platform sandals. No wonder Mom wore running shoes half the time, Sarah told herself. She decided that she was going to keep the sandals in her closet and haul them out the next time her mother complained about the styles that Sarah and her friends liked.

A group of kids was standing near the refreshment table and several more were gathered out in the lobby, some just talking and others waiting for their rides to pick them up. Derek, however, was nowhere to be seen.

Micki had been talking on the pay phone, no doubt calling her mother to drive her and Rick home. "Derek gave me a message for you," she said as Sarah approached. "He said he's tired of being walked out on."

That sounded familiar. David had said the same thing last night, Sarah reflected. This double identity business was definitely tough on relationships.

The only one who seemed to be enjoying it was Rick. "I thought your sister Sarah was a fruitcake," he confided to Sarah. "But I see now that you're just as bad."

"Thanks a lot," Sarah snapped.

"Think nothing of it," Rick cracked. "I'm a master of flattery. Actually, I kind of like girls who are a little bit flaky."

Sarah had no transportation, so she had to ask Micki for a lift. On the drive home, she did her best to ignore Rick's wisecracks. But there was no question that he was flirting with her.

Sarah was relieved when Mrs. Davis finally let her off at her house. She ran through the garage, stopping just long enough to change back to her own identity, and hurried to her room.

Micki had whispered in the car that she was going to call as soon as she had a chance to talk in private. Sarah dragged the extension from the hall into her room and shut the door. When Micki called, she picked it up on the first ring.

"How could any evening start out so great and end up being such a total disaster!" Sarah wailed. For almost ten minutes she regaled Micki with a blow-by-blow account of her problems.

When she finished, Micki was silent for a long time. Finally, she said, "Sarah, not that I'm not interested in all the details of your adventures. But I'm getting tired of playing sidekick. You never even bothered to ask me how my evening went. You never asked how I got along with Rick."

"Rick! Give me a break," Sarah said. "You can do better than him any day."

"That didn't stop you from flirting with him in the car on the way home," Micki pointed out.

Sarah was outraged. "I didn't flirt with him! He was flirting with me!"

"Same difference," Micki said infuriatingly.

Sarah felt betrayed. Ever since she had discovered she was a witch, she had been thinking of how to use her powers on Micki's behalf. "Look at all the spells I used to find you the perfect boyfriend," she reminded her friend. "I admit, none of them worked very well. But that wasn't my fault."

Micki sighed. "Great. I appreciate your effort. But if you were my real friend, you'd accept my right to find my own boyfriend. Even if he doesn't turn out to be Mr. Perfect."

Before Sarah could answer, Micki hung up.

Sarah pulled on her bathrobe and found a paperback to read in bed. She knew she wasn't going to have an easy time sleeping. Tomorrow night her parents and Nicole were due back from San Francisco. She had less than twenty-four hours to straighten out Nicole's life.

And while I'm at it, Sarah told herself, I'd better try to do something about my own.

Chapter 12

Miss Ramsey lived in an old gingerbread Victorian house up on a hill overlooking the river and Harper's Landing Park. A lot of the houses in that neighborhood had been renovated, but Miss Ramsey's looked as if nothing had been changed since the day the first inhabitant moved in almost a hundred years before. It was exactly the kind of old house that Sarah had seen in horror movies, complete with cupolas and turrets and the kind of cobwebby attic windows that make you wonder whether there aren't ghosts inside, looking out.

"Spooky, isn't it?" asked Betsy Fields, as she stood on the sidewalk next to Sarah, surveying the house with suspicion. "To look at this old place, you'd think it belonged to some mean old witch. Not an ordinary high school phys-ed teacher like Miss Ramsey."

Sarah couldn't help smiling. If only Betsy knew that the real witch's house in Waterview was the Connell family's spic and span white frame house!

Of course, Betsy had no idea that Sarah Connell was an apprentice witch. At the moment, she didn't even realize which Connell sister she was talking to.

Reluctantly, Sarah had used one of the last precious drops of her magic potion to transform herself into Nicole for the cheerleaders' Sunday brunch. She was pretty sure that being squad captain was the last thing Nicole would want, especially if it meant losing Derek, and she was determined to head off Stephanie Clarke before she did any more campaigning.

Sarah rang the bell, and Miss Ramsey showed her and Betsy inside. Several other early arrivals were seated in the living room on a maroon velvet couch with carved lion's paws for legs. The room itself was enormous, almost large enough to hold a small school dance in.

That was a good thing, Sarah decided, considering the amount of junk lying around. To begin with, there was twice as much furniture as any one house needed — huge mahogany chests and tables, two or three layers of rugs, and vases and knickknacks covering every surface. But the normal furniture was just the beginning. In every corner of the room there were piles of belongings — books, papers, sewing gear, a tennis racket, even lumber and tools from some project that had been begun weeks or even months earlier and never finished.

Several of these piles of junk had become nests for Miss Ramsey's cats. Gray, ginger, calico, white — the coach seemed to have cats of every variety, all of whom surveyed the visiting cheerleaders with a notable lack of enthusiasm.

Betsy Fields managed to find one self-satisfied-looking tabby who actually seemed interested in having its chin scratched. "I love cats," she enthused to Miss Ramsey. "How many do you have?"

The coach looked as if she'd been asked a tough question. "About ten," she said vaguely.

"Oh," said Betsy. She wasn't sure how anyone could not know *exactly* how many cats they owned, but she didn't want to seem rude by asking.

Miss Ramsey didn't seem to notice anything odd in Betsy's reaction. "This place is quite a local landmark," she said, changing the subject. "I'm planning to renovate it, but unfortunately I don't seem to have as much time as I need."

Minutes later she was happily telling the group the house's history. "It's one of the oldest houses in Waterview," she explained. "The original owners were the two Sharp sisters, Neddy and Serafina, who lived here for many years."

According to Miss Ramsey, both sisters had been in love with a man who was a captain on a clipper ship. The captain loved Neddy, but he wanted her to travel around the world with him on his ship. She refused because she didn't like sailing.

"So the captain proposed to Serafina," Miss Ramsey concluded. "They left on their first round-the-world voyage the day after the wedding. And they never came back. The ship sank somewhere in the Pacific. Neddy never married after that. She spent the rest of her life as a hermit in this house."

Sarah sighed. "What a romantic story!"

"I'm not so sure about that," Betsy said. "I wouldn't waste *my* life pining away for some man who married my sister instead of me!"

"I guess not," Sarah agreed. Betsy's comment made her wonder how Nicole would feel if she knew that her little sister had been seeing Derek in her place.

By now the rest of the squad had arrived, and Miss Ramsey urged them to help themselves to the buffet table. All the food was good, even though it was a rather strange assortment of items. There were cold cuts, scrambled eggs, some kind of Chinese noodle dish, a hot baking dish filled with beef enchiladas, potato salad, and various other foods that didn't seem to belong together.

Eric Rissom, in line just ahead of Sarah, was happily filling his plate with a little of everything.

"Poor Miss Ramsey," he said, shaking his head. "She means well, but I don't think planning is her strong suit. I bet she's been cooking all week. She didn't have to make all this food just for us."

Sarah decided that Eric was right. Miss Ramsey was absent-minded and nervous a lot of the time, but basically warm-hearted. Unfortunately, she was also a little naive, since it never occurred to her that Candy Sweet wasn't the devoted student she pretended to be.

Bravely, Sarah decided to reward Miss Ramsey's efforts by sampling her enchiladas. While she was serving herself a good-sized helping, Stephanie Clarke came up behind her. "It's all set," Stephanie whispered. "I called some of the other girls last night, and I think there are enough votes for you to beat out Candy."

Sarah's heart sank. What was she going to

do now? Stalling for time, she took a small bite of her enchilada. "Look, Steph. I thought it over, and I'm not sure. . . ."

Before she could finish her sentence, Sarah felt a wave of fire radiating through her mouth. She liked hot Mexican food, but Miss Ramsey's was the three-alarm kind.

Sarah opened her mouth to ask for a glass of water. Instead, what came out was a strangled, high pitched hiccup. "Hu — ick!"

Eric and a couple of the senior girls laughed.

"Drink a glass of water in one gulp, then put your head between your knees," someone suggested.

"No, no. You've got to blow into a paper bag," someone else said.

Everyone crowded around contributing their own favorite hiccup remedies, but none of them did a bit of good. Sarah was mortified. She used to have this reaction to hot foods when she was younger, but it hadn't happened in years. Instead of going away, her hiccups seemed to get louder and sillier-sounding by the minute.

Worst of all, the hiccuping seemed to be loosening her hold on Nicole's identity. Sarah could feel the familiar tingling in her feet and hands that was a signal that she was about to change back into her own body.

Talk about disasters! she warned herself.

What could be worse than having her secret revealed in front of the entire cheerleading squad of Waterview High?

It got so bad that Sarah finally asked Miss Ramsey for directions to the bathroom, which was up on the second floor of the house. Locking herself in, she tried holding her breath and taking deep drinks of water to cure her hiccuping attacks. Fortunately, the attack subsided and so did the warning signs that she was losing her grip on her impersonation of Nicole.

Sarah was on her way back downstairs when she realized that Candy Sweet and her friend Mona Fisher were standing in the alcove behind the staircase having a private conversation. Mona had long, black hair that she wore parted on one side so that a mane of hair hung down over the left eye. Mona considered this look glamorous, and a lot of guys seemed to agree. But Sarah could never look at Mona without being reminded of a horse wearing blinkers — or at least, half a set of blinkers.

When it came to her friendship with Candy, Mona was definitely Number Two, though. No matter what Candy did, Mona always seemed to be there at her side, flattering her and agreeing with every word she said. Sarah couldn't help wondering whether Mona behaved the same way when there was no one around but she and Candy. Although she knew eavesdropping was wrong, she couldn't resist the temptation to listen in.

"I think this food is totally gross," Mona was saying. "Have you ever heard of serving potato salad with Chinese food?"

Candy answered by pretending to stick her finger down her throat. "And this house is a mess," she added. "Old Ramsey certainly is a slob. My mom would never let the cleaning lady leave stuff lying around like this."

Sarah was about to come to Miss Ramsey's defense. Renovating a house was always messy, and she was pretty sure that Miss Ramsey didn't have a cleaning lady to do her chores for her. Besides, it was mean to call Miss Ramsey a slob behind her back after she had gone to so much trouble to entertain them.

But before Sarah could confront them, Candy and Mona changed the subject.

"Can you believe that Nicole Connell, of all people, is thinking of running against me for captain?" Candy sniffed. "I don't know what's gotten into her. I never thought she'd have the nerve."

"Nicole knows the captain's job always goes to a senior," Mona agreed. "But then, what can you expect from a girl who wears penny loafers!"

"Right," echoed Candy. "Nicole and her high standards! She thinks she's better than the rest of us. She thinks she's better than *all* the rest of us. I'm in her chemistry class, and do you know that she wouldn't even give me the answers to the last test we had? She *said* it was because she doesn't believe in cheating, but I'm sure she was just jealous. She wants me to fail."

Good for Nicole, Sarah thought. Candy cheated so much that she thought the rest of the school owed her the answers to every test. Nicole was probably the only kid who had ever had the nerve to turn Candy down. No doubt that was why Candy had tripped her in practice yesterday.

"I wouldn't worry about this election," Mona reassured Candy. "When push comes to shove, Nicole will never go through with it. I bet that if someone does nominate her, she'll withdraw her name before we have a chance to vote."

That was exactly what Sarah had been planning to do. Now, of course, she would have cut out her tongue before she would give Mona the satisfaction of being right.

Stomping down the stairs, she confronted the two girls, her eyes ablaze with indignation. "I'll have you know that Nicole Connell is no quitter. She's going to go through with running for captain whether you like it or not."

Candy flicked her long hair over one shoulder and regarded Sarah with cool disdain. "What's this 'she' business? I thought only royalty referred to itself in the third person."

Sarah knew she had made a mistake, but she was in no mood to be corrected by Candy. "Since when are you an expert on grammar?" she shot back.

Maybe the remark wouldn't go down in history as one of the wittiest ever, but it did get a laugh from Mona.

Candy glanced at her friend reprovingly. "What's wrong with you? Nothing's funny. If you're supposed to laugh, I'll let you know."

"Sorry," Mona said. She was used to being bullied by Candy, but her tone of voice said that this time her friend had gone too far.

When Sarah got back to the living room, most of the squad had finished their food, and the business meeting was getting underway. Betsy Fields gave a report on the state of the equipment fund, and Miss Ramsey talked about the possibility of the cheerleaders sponsoring a dance to raise money. Finally it was time for new business.

Stephanie Clarke stood up. "I move we vote this year by secret ballot."

Naturally, Candy spoke against Stephanie's

motion. "I don't t
she said. "I mean,
hide, right?"

"So much for the
"I'm sure if our cou
exposed to Candy's
would have written
pletely differently."

After that, Stephanie　　　　　　by a
wide margin. Mona nom　　　Candy for captain. To Sarah's surprise, Tanya Rinaldi, one
of the senior cheerleaders, nominated Nicole.

At the last minute, Sarah realized that she
and Candy were each expected to make a short
speech. That, she thought, was more than any
girl should have to do for her sister. Nicole was
good at this sort of thing, but Sarah always felt
her knees turning to jelly when she had to
speak in front of a group.

This time, the fact that everyone in her audience thought she was Nicole gave her courage. "I know it's traditional for this honor to
go to a senior," she said. "And normally I'm
not against tradition. I just thought the squad
ought to have a chance to vote for the person
who's willing to work the hardest. And, uh, I
promise that if I'm elected, I'll work very hard
to deserve your confidence."

nto applause, and Sarah sat ... ks burning from the effort of ... k confident.

... had waited to speak last. "I don't need ... troduce myself," she said. "You all know ... e. And I'm sure you know I'm chairman of the Spring Carnival, too." Candy looked around the room pointedly, just to make sure that everyone had grasped the implications of her remark.

"I know a threat when I hear it," Eric muttered under his breath as he fished a pencil out of his shirt pocket to mark his ballot. "But with a secret ballot, how's Candy ever going to know who voted against her?"

Sarah figured she had upheld Nicole's honor by keeeping her in the running. On the other hand, she still wasn't all that sure she wanted Nicole to actually win. After staring down at her own blank ballot in confusion, she impulsively wrote in Candy's name. As much as she disliked her opponent, Candy's winning would save her a lot of explaining.

Betsy Fields collected the ballots, and she and Miss Ramsey counted them. "It looks as if we have a clear winner," the coach announced. "Nicole Connell has sixteen votes."

"Right," Betsy added unnecessarily. "And Candy Sweet got two votes."

One or two people gasped in surprise, and everyone's eyes went automatically to Mona Fisher.

"Hey, gang. Wait!" Mona said without thinking. "I voted for Nicole. Honest."

"Even I am amazed at how well our little scheme worked," Stephanie told Nicole as they and Eric left the brunch together. "I knew quite a few kids on the squad were tired of being bossed around by Candy. But I never dreamed you would win almost unanimously."

"What I'd love to know," Eric put in, "is who voted for Candy. That was a stroke of genius, in a way. Now she can't retaliate against any one of us without wondering if she's trying to get revenge on the one person who was on her side."

Sarah giggled. "I confess. I know it's dumb, but I had a crisis of confidence and voted for Candy at the last minute. But don't tell her," she begged.

Stephanie laughed. "Your secret's safe with us. I think it'll be a lot more fun to keep Candy guessing for the rest of the year."

Chapter 13

Sarah couldn't decide how she felt about the election. Part of her felt proud of what she had accomplished. No matter how much of a pain Nicole could be at times, she would make a much better cheerleading captain than Candy Sweet!

But another part of Sarah was convinced that she had just ruined her sister's life. She was pretty sure that Derek would take Nicole's election as a signal that their relationship was over. Not that she cared! Cute as Derek was, she couldn't imagine letting a guy dictate to her what she should do. Nicole might not see it that way, however, and Sarah wasn't looking forward to seeing her sister's reaction when she learned that Derek was breaking up with her.

Worse yet, Sarah hadn't figured out how she

was going to deal with the fact Nicole was bound to find out that her friends had been seeing her around town all weekend, while she was actually in San Francisco.

Naturally, Sarah told herself, there had to be a spell that would take care of revising Nicole's memory so that she would never suspect. But she had no idea what the spell would be.

It was a few minutes after noon when Sarah left Miss Ramsey's house, and her folks' plane was due back a little before midnight. That meant that she had less than twelve hours to straighten out the mess that it had taken her two and a half days to make. If her aunt Pam didn't step in and help her out, and *soon*, she was going to be in big trouble!

The potion she had dabbed on that morning to change herself into Nicole was already wearing off by the time Sarah got to her aunt Pam's. She rang the bell and her aunt appeared, dressed in pleated corduroy trousers, knee-high boots made of embossed leather, and a green silk shirt with dramatic full sleeves.

Sarah was filled with admiration. "You look wonderful!" she enthused.

Aunt Pam smiled. "Thanks. I wish I could say the same for you, but I'm afraid your look isn't quite . . . shall we say, pulled together."

She let Sarah in and led her to the mirror in

the back room. Sarah was dismayed to see that once again the left side side of her hair had reverted to its normal chestnut shade while the hair on the right side was still Nicole's, as blonde and straight as cornsilk.

"You remind of that woman in the Charles Addams cartoons," Aunt Pam observed. "I always thought his work was very unfair to witches. Of course, seeing you now, I wonder if he didn't know at least *something* about witch's hair. . . ."

Sarah sipped a cup of her aunt's cinnamon flavored tea while she reported on her activities since she was last at the shop. "I'm starting to feel desperate," she concluded. "I need some new magic spells. One to make Nicole accept what's happened while she was away. And another one for Derek. You know, a love potion to make him forget that he's upset with Nicole."

Aunt Pam got up from the table and started rummaging through an old cedar chest that stood in the corner of her living room. When she returned she was carrying an old-fashioned fountain pen.

"I think I can help you deal with Nicole's memory," she said. "This is the same magic pen I used when I attended the audition in your mother's place, back when we were both in high school. All I have to do is make up a special batch of ink to use with it."

Aunt Pam went downstairs to her ground floor teashop to collect the ingredients she needed for the ink, returning a few minutes later with her arms full of strange-looking roots and herbs, as well as a long plug of licorice candy, from which she broke off pieces for Sarah and herself to chew.

"I assume Nicole keeps a diary," she said.

Sarah nodded. "She makes a big deal of it, too. She seems to think we're all dying to sneak a peek at it. Personally, I couldn't care less."

"That's good. I mean, it's good that she keeps one."

Aunt Pam had tied a full-length apron over her clothes and she was busily mixing the ink ingredients in a small copper pot. "Here's what you have to do. Find a way to get your hands on that diary. Then make the entries for this weekend in magic ink. You can write directly over what Nicole put down. Her entries will disappear and what you've written will be there in its place."

Sarah stared at the tea leaves in the bottom of her empty cup. "Isn't that a little bit drastic? I mean, it's as if I'm rewriting Nicole's life."

Aunt Pam frowned. "You've already rewritten her life. Now everyone will have to think it was the way *you* lived it. You should have thought of that before you started this little project."

"I didn't mean any harm," Sarah vowed. "And I promise I'll never do anything like this again."

"I hope not," Aunt Pam said, shaking her head. "For one thing, I'm not as good at mixing up these potions as I used to be. We modern witches don't bother much with these old spells. We prefer natural methods, you know."

"I certainly hope you can help me with a love potion," Sarah said, watching her aunt as she measured out more herbs and spices for the ink. "I have a feeling I'm going to need a really good one to get Derek to come back to Nicole."

"I'm afraid I can't help you there."

Sarah's mouth dropped open. "What do you mean, you can't help?"

Aunt Pam took off her apron and sat down across from Sarah. "If you recall, your last experiments with love didn't turn out too well. Not only did you change your mind about Cody Rice, but the boys you lined up for your friend Micki weren't exactly suitable."

Sarah blushed, thinking of her well-meaning attempts to find the perfect boy for her best friend.

"Okay," she admitted, "I made a few mistakes. But I still need a potion."

"I'm afraid I can't give you one," Aunt Pam said. "There are some things that even apprentice witches have to work out on their own."

As Sarah left Aunt Pam's she ran into Micki standing at the front door of the shop.

"What are you doing here?" she asked.

"Would you believe it if I told you that I needed some herb tea and was hoping your aunt's shop would be open on a Sunday?" Micki volunteered.

"No way. For one thing, you don't like herb tea," Sarah pointed out.

"Okay. Then I'll tell the truth. I was coming to talk to your aunt because I'm worried about you."

Sarah was touched. Despite their quarrels this weekend, Micki was still looking out for her. "You really are a good friend," she said, giving Micki a big hug. "I don't deserve it, either. You were right about my being selfish. I ruined your date because I was so wrapped up in my own problems."

Micki waved her hand. "Forget it. We'll talk about that stuff later. I just thought you might need some help, considering Nicole is coming back tonight."

"Do I ever!" Sarah admitted. As they walked briskly in the direction of their own neighborhood, Sarah filled Micki in on what had happened at the cheerleaders' brunch.

"Sounds great," Micki said. "Especially since Aunt Pam has given you a way to fool Nicole into thinking she did it all herself. So what's the problem?"

"The problem is Derek," Sarah told her. "He'll be furious. He wanted me — I mean, he wanted Nicole — to quit cheerleading completely."

Micki wrinkled her nose. "Gross! Why would any boy want that? You'd think he'd be proud to be dating a girl who's a cheerleader."

Sarah had a theory about that. "Something tells me that Derek isn't as confident as he seems. I think he just wants Nicole to pay more attention to him."

Micki was quiet for a long time. "Boys are so confusing," she said finally. "I mean, if a girl *wants* to spend a lot of time with a boy, he acts as if she's chasing him. . . ."

Sarah stopped in her tracks and grabbed her friend by the shoulders. "Micki, you're brilliant!" she exclaimed. "Absolutely brilliant!"

"I am?" Micki blinked in confusion. "What did I say?"

"You just gave me an idea of how to change

Derek's mind," Sarah told her. "And it won't take any magic potions at all. Aunt Pam was right. All I need to solve this particular problem is a little practical psychology."

Derek seemed surprised but pleased to get a phone call from Nicole asking him to meet her that afternoon in Harper's Landing Park.

Sarah, transformed into Nicole for what she hoped was the last time, bicycled to the park, wearing her own turquoise jogging suit, an outfit that always made her feel energetic and confident. Even so, by the time she reached the pond-side gazebo where she had asked Derek to meet her, she was feeling a little shaky. Her idea for changing Derek's mind had sounded like a sure thing when she explained it to Micki. Now she wasn't so confident.

The gazebo was a white wrought-iron pavilion surrounded by graceful weeping willow trees and overlooking a small pond. Sarah had always thought the spot the most romantic place in town, and the knowledge that she was actually going to be meeting a boy there made her stomach do nervous flip-flops.

Derek's arrival only made her more nervous still. It was a cool morning, and Derek was wearing a light-blue windbreaker that accentuated his tanned good looks. His smile seemed even more dazzling than usual. Even that cute dimple in the middle of his cleft chin was unusually noticeable. Once again, with Derek near, Sarah had no trouble figuring out what her sister saw in him.

As Derek fastened the lock on his bike, Sarah practically flew to his side. "Derek, darling!" she gushed, clinging to his arm.

He looked startled. "What's up?"

"Why, I wanted to tell you my decision, of course," Sarah said, batting her eyes outrageously. "I've decided I *will* give up cheerleading for you after all."

"You will?" Derek sounded shocked and not altogether pleased. The truth was, he had asked Nicole to quit the squad because he wanted her to prove she cared about him. Now that she was willing to do just that, he wasn't sure he liked the idea.

"Of course," Sarah prattled on. "It was the *least* I could do. The only reason I hesitated to give you my answer at all was that it's such a big step for the two of us to be taking."

"It is?" Derek knew he sounded idiotic. But the truth was, he hadn't any idea what Nicole was talking about. The only thing he knew for sure was that he didn't like the direction the conversation was taking.

"Do you think we should talk to your parents

this afternoon?" Sarah went on. "I mean, I know we're young to think about getting officially engaged. But our folks ought to at least know about our plans."

The word 'engaged' worked like magic to restore Derek's power of speech. "What plans?" he stammered out. "We don't have any plans. And who said anything about being engaged?"

Sarah did her best to look innocent. Luckily, Nicole's big, blue eyes made her task easy. Very slowly, as if talking to a kindergarten child, she explained her reasoning.

"If I'm going to quit cheerleading for you, that means we'll be going to all the games together, right? And that mean's we'll be going steady for the rest of our time in high school, right? And I certainly wouldn't make that kind of commitment unless we were going to get engaged and married after graduation."

Sarah batted her eyelashes a few extra times for good measure and gazed into Derek's eyes. "That *is* what you had in mind, isn't it?"

Derek looked completely panic-stricken. "Not exactly. . . ."

He looked so pained, that Sarah was starting to feel truly sorry for him. "Are you saying that you don't want to get engaged?" she asked, as if the thought hadn't occurred to her until that minute.

"Well, to be honest, no."

Sarah turned away and gazed soulfully out over the pond. "I guess I'll have to live with your decision. But of course, that means that my promise is called off, too. I won't be quitting the squad."

"That's okay." Derek put in quickly. "You're really understanding, Nicole. I really appreciate this. I'll think of a way to make it up to you, honest I will."

"Do me one favor, okay?" Sarah said. "Let's just forget about this conversation, okay? It would upset me too much to talk about this again." Sarah did her best to look grief-stricken as she rested her cheek against Derek's shoulder.

"Sure, sure," he agreed. "I know just how you feel."

Before she and Derek parted, Sarah actually managed to squeeze out a few tears. She cried just enough to make her performance completely convincing, but not so much that her eyes would look red and puffy, ruining her appearance.

I really should think about a career as an actress, she told herself as she pedaled her bike back home. If that performance were on film, it would have won an Academy Award.

Chapter 14

"You should have seen Derek's face when I mentioned going to talk to his parents!" Sarah told Micki when she got back from the park. "I thought he was going to pass out on the spot. Seriously."

Micki laughed. "I wish I could have been there to see it. Didn't you have a hard time keeping a straight face?"

"I don't think I could have done it if I had been saying those things on my own behalf," Sarah confessed. "But somehow it's easier when I'm being Nicole. It's like wearing a disguise. I feel a lot more relaxed because if I mess up, no one will know that Sarah Connell was responsible."

"That's too bad, in a way," Micki said. "You still have to straighten things out with David, and you can only do that as Sarah."

David!

Sarah had almost forgotten about him. She had been so busy trying to fix up Nicole's life that she had scarcely given a thought to her own boyfriend all weekend. Fortunately, David worked on Saturdays, so he hadn't expected to see her. But usually he and Sarah at least talked on the phone. This weekend, even if David had decided to call her to make up, Sarah wouldn't have been around to talk to him.

"I suppose I'd better see David this afternoon and work things out," Sarah said. "But before I go over to his house looking for him, I'd better change back into my own body."

She reached into the pocket of her warm-up pants, fishing for her vial of *Transformation* potion. This time, she realized almost immediately that the small glass container was gone.

"I can hardly believe it!" Micki said disgustedly. "I can see you losing that stuff once. But twice! Where is your mind?"

"I don't understand it myself," Sarah said. "Except that I was in such a good mood about the way things worked out with Derek that I wasn't paying much attention. Anyway, we'd better retrace the route I took from the park. That potion could easily fall into the wrong hands."

After stopping at Micki's house to pick up her bike, the two of them began slowly covering the street Sarah had taken to her meeting with Derek. They were poking their way up Elm Street, studying the leaf-stuffed gutters when Tina Jordan came by.

Tina was surprised to see Micki with Sarah's big sister Nicole. "What's up?" she asked. "Where's Sarah?"

"Oh, she's around." Sarah said vaguely. To her satisfaction, she noted that her voice was dripping with boredom. If this experiment went on any longer she was going to end up being every bit as stuck-up as Nicole.

Still confused, Tina rested her bike against the curb and watched their efforts with curiosity. "Lose something?"

"Oh, no," Sarah lied.

"That's okay, then," Tina said. "I thought you might be looking for that little glass bottle I saw just up the block."

"Where?" Sarah and Micki shouted in unison.

Tina pointed up the street. The girls spotted the vial just in time to see that the rubber stopper had come out, and the last few drops of potion had made a tiny spot on the pavement. As they watched, a shaggy mutt trotting down the sidewalk made a detour out into the street to check out the spill. The mutt sniffed at the wet spot, then gave it a few cautious licks.

In a flash, the bedraggled, tired-looking dog was transformed. Leaping high into the air, it gave a yelp of joy and darted down the street. By the time the mutt hit the corner it had sprouted long ears, longer legs, and a beautifully groomed poodle coat.

"What got into him?" wondered Tina. Luckily, though, she had looked away to adjust her bike's gears before the poodle fur began to pop out.

Micki clapped a hand over her mouth. The loss of the potion might be a disaster. Even so, she had all she could do to stifle a fit of giggles.

Later, back at the Connell kitchen, Micki tried to make Sarah see the bright side of the situation. "At least now we know what a dog daydreams about," she pointed out. "I wouldn't want to be a poodle myself. I think if I could be any breed I'd be a golden retriever. . . ."

"Can't you ever be serious!" Sarah snapped. "My potion is gone. Finished. And so am I."

Micki opened the refrigerator and started sampling the healthy snacks that Mrs. Connell had left for Sarah and Simon. "I don't get it," she said between mouthfuls of carrot cake. "You'll just change back into your own body gradually. That's what happened before, right?"

"Right," Sarah said glumly. "But it's been three hours now since I used that potion and it hasn't even started wearing off yet. It seems like every time I use it, the stuff lasts longer."

Micki shrugged. "Then you've got to make the change happen yourself. You did it before without any potion. That's how all this started."

Sarah knew Micki was right, but for some reason it had been easier for her to start being Nicole than it was for her to go back to being her true self.

"Maybe that's because you don't know who you really are," Micki suggested.

"Give me a break!" Micki's idea sounded like something her father would say, Sarah thought. She knew perfectly well who she was. She was Sarah Connell, Nicole's impulsive, slightly scatter-brained younger sister. Other than that, her only claim to distinction was being an apprentice witch. But unfortunately, she couldn't tell anyone about that. It was just her luck that the one quality she had worth bragging about had to be kept secret.

After Micki left, Sarah went up to Nicole's room and starting rummaging around her bureau. She was pretty sure Nicole had packed so fast for the weekend that she had forgotten to take her diary with her. And sure enough, there it was, hidden in her top drawer under a pile of nightgowns.

Sarah stared down guiltily at the red leather diary. Even though Aunt Pam had told her this was the only way to make Nicole forget that she had not been home all weekend, she didn't like the thought of messing around with her sister's diary. It seemed wrong.

Of course, Sarah rationalized, at the moment she was still Nicole . . . in a way. At least she looked like Nicole. So why shouldn't she read her diary?

The thought made her smile. Crossing her fingers, she wished that the diary's lock would open. The tiny gold keyhole turned slowly and the book popped open. Sarah got out the magic pen and ink she had been given and started to work.

Thursday night's entry, where Nicole mentioned the trip, was easy to get rid of. Sarah just wrote what Aunt Pam had told her to put down, and the old entry made by Nicole vanished magically. Then Sarah went on to fill in the entries for the rest of the weekend. She wrote about going to the movies on Friday, her date for the dance with Derek, and getting elected cheerleading captain.

When she finished, Sarah began leafing back

through the old entries. No matter how tempted she was, it seemed wrong to read a lot of what her sister had written. But when she saw her own name on one page she decided she was entitled to know what her sister thought about her.

Sarah is so immature! the entry began. *Yesterday she came down to breakfast wearing a green outfit that looked like a hospital scrub suit. It was gross! Tracy asked me later in the day if Sarah had escaped from a hospital. I was so embarrassed. . . .*

Frowning, Sarah turned the page.

Still, I've got to admire Sarah, Nicole went on. *I'm always worrying about what people will think, and sometimes I have trouble standing up for myself. Not Sarah! She has spunk. When she wants something, she goes after it. I really admire her.*

Sarah felt tears welling up in her eyes. She had never imagined that Nicole would ever say something that nice about her. Of course, strictly speaking, Nicole hadn't said it. But at least she'd thought it.

All I want right now, Sarah told herself, is to be me again.

Closing the diary with a sigh, Sarah went back to her own room. Her folks were due back in a couple of hours. She had no idea what she'd do if she didn't manage the change by then.

Sarah felt panicky and a little bit ill. But at the same time she couldn't stop herself from yawning. She hadn't slept well all weekend. Trying to juggle two lives certainly took up a lot of energy.

At the last minute, just before closing her eyes, she reached up and switched off her bedside lamp.

The next thing Sarah knew, she was awakened by the sound of footsteps in the hall. At first she thought it must be Simon, but then she heard voices. Unless Simon had starting talking to himself, she could rule him out.

Burglars!

Sarah sat up in bed. Her room was pitch black. If she kept the light off, maybe the burglars would assume she was asleep.

Then a terrible realization occurred to her, even worse than having burglars in the house, if possible. The voices she heard belonged to her parents and Nicole, back from the weekend.

Sarah was glad she had turned her light out. If her parents realized there were two Nicoles in the house and no Sarah they'd probably have heart attacks on the spot.

Suddenly, the noises sorted themselves out. Sarah could make out her mom's voice, just outside her bedroom door. "I'll just take a peek in on Sarah to make sure she's all right."

Before Sarah had a chance to duck under the covers, the door to her room swung open. A shaft of light from the hallway fell across Sarah's bed, almost blinding her.

"What's going on?" her mother asked worriedly.

Sarah couldn't think of a thing to say. "Huh?" she mumbled. "Is something going on?"

"Well, of course, dear," her mother said. "You don't normally sit up in bed with no lights on, do you?" Kate Connell came over to the bed and gave her daughter a kiss on the forehead. "Lie down and try to sleep. You must have had a bad dream. We'll tell you about our trip tomorrow."

When her mom had gone, Sarah turned on the light and checked herself out in the mirror. No wonder her mother hadn't noticed anything! She was herself again.

The next morning, it almost seemed as if the weekend had been a dream.

Before homeroom, Sarah went around to

David's locker, intending to apologize. "I'm sorry about this weekend," she began. "I know I acted strange, but I had a lot of homework to do."

David smiled down at her. "Is that all? I thought something was seriously wrong."

Sarah gulped. "What a ridiculous idea."

"I know," David admitted. "You won't believe this, but I was jealous. I had this crazy idea that you liked Derek. I don't know why."

"Derek! You mean the hulk?" Sarah laughed, and David joined in. Some things were just too ridiculous to be worth discussing.

That evening at dinner, Nicole described at length how she'd been elected squad captain at the cheerleaders' brunch.

Listening to the story, Mr. and Mrs. Connell looked vaguely confused. They knew there was something wrong with Nicole's version of the weekend, but their own minds were foggy. The trip to San Francisco was already vague in their minds, as if it had happened a long time ago.

Naturally, Nicole couldn't finish any dinner-table discussion without getting in a dig at her sister.

"It's too bad you don't go out for more school activities," she said, looking at Sarah. "Simon and I were really active, even when we were freshmen like you. All you ever do is hang around with Micki. And that doofus, David."

Normally that dig would have made Sarah see red. But this evening she stayed cool. "I am plenty active," she said mysteriously. "I have activities you don't even know about."

Mr. and Mrs. Connell exchanged questioning glances, and Simon raised one eyebrow in amusement. Nicole took the bait. "What's that supposed to mean?" she demanded.

"Oh, nothing." For once, Sarah was enjoying being the one to tease Nicole, not the other way around.

After a pause, Sarah added, "All I meant was, you can't really know a person until you've walked a mile in their shoes."

Kate Connell beamed her approval. "That's true dear. I guess you're really growing up."

Later that evening, while going through her school notebook, Nicole came upon the note that Mr. Connell had written to the principal to excuse her from school on Friday. Nicole studied the note for a long time. "Please excuse my daughter from school today," it said.

Nicole didn't recall Sarah being absent on Friday. For that matter, *she* couldn't exactly remember being at school that day, either. She looked across the living room at Sarah, who was trying to listen to French vocabulary through the earphones of her portable cassette player while watching MTV. Nicole couldn't help thinking that something strange had happened this weekend and that Sarah knew something about it.

"Sometimes," Nicole said out loud, "I think my sister has even more secrets than she lets on. I wonder if I'll ever find out what they are."

Sarah pretended not to hear, but inside she was delighted. For once, Nicole had admitted that her younger sister might know something she didn't. More important than that, Sarah had a new picture of Nicole's life, which she had always thought was so perfect. Now she knew that Nicole worked hard, had to deal with turkeys like Candy, and had a boyfriend who wasn't the brightest.

Sarah's own life looked pretty good. She had Micki and David, and she was, most incredibly, a teen witch. She just had to try to keep her powers under better control.

Live and learn, Sarah thought. Everything would turn out fine . . . wouldn't it?